domino

DOMINO BOOKS LIMITED

Some people seem to think that it's just a matter of setting yourself up as a detective or even a shyster lawyer and before you can say Philip Marlowe there's a piece sashaying in from the waiting room just as you're buying yourself a short one from the office bottle and although she's got a figure to beat the band her eyes are shy and only slightly sinful, like two kisses in a cathedral.

But after you've lit your pipe and wisecracked for a while and heard about her little sister who went out for a manicure and finished up in Mexico, you know she's a cold man-eating broad who figures you for a fall-guy.

THE LAST PRIVATE EYE IN BELFAST

By

MIKE SHELLEY

The Last Private Eye in Belfast
is an original publication of Domino Books Ltd,
Edenderry Industrial Estate,
326/328 Crumlin Rd, Belfast BT14 7EE

ISBN 0 946963 00 2

Typeset, printed and bound in Northern Ireland by
Brough, Cox and Dunn Ltd, Clifton St, Belfast.
Set in 10 on 12 Century Textbook.

Cover and Design by Triplicate,
Linenhall St, Belfast
Illustration by Tony Bell

Chapter 1
Portuguese Joe

Before the full extent of Portuguese Joe's depravity was known or even imagined, he was fond of saying to anyone who hinted otherwise that his business activities were 'entirely above board'.

It was in O'Brian's Gin Palace that I first heard him make this claim. After nearly choking on the last of my whiskey I suggested that in his case the board was pitched at a conveniently low level, if not lying solidly on the ground.

Joe gave a condescending smile and reminded me that whereas I had occasionally found it necessary to put the minds of police detectives at rest, he had never yet found himself in that embarrassing position. And this was such a sore point with me that, forgetting it was his turn to buy a round, I made a few choice comments on other, more intimate positions he had been in, and left the snug doors flapping as I pushed through them on my way to the street.

If I hadn't been in such a hurry I might even have asked him why such an upstanding citizen like himself should be known throughout his native Belfast as Portuguese Joe, a distinctly spivish name if there ever was one.

Surely, I might have remarked, it couldn't derive from the 'practical joke' he played on the countryfolk of Donegal by posing as a curate. I would have expressed no doubts whatsoever that every penny of the substantial collections he took 'to nourish the poor babies of Portugal' and 'to help convert the heathen Welsh' was remitted to where it would do the most good.

I might even have listened to his own version of the name's origin, which relates his rise to power as a political protégé of Salazar in the Lisbon of the early sixties. However, as I found out from his father whom I plied with drink one evening in Robinson's Bar, the only time Joe visited Europe was in 1963 when he was on the run after seducing and impregnating a sixteen year old Belfast schoolgirl. Pleading poverty, he gained admittance to a French monastery where he lay doggo for several months. It couldn't have been easy for him.

As it happened, that meeting in O'Brian's was the last I saw of my Iberian adversary for some time. Then, one morning in late June as I was strolling towards my offices, I decided to call into the Ajax Cafe for a cup of tea.

Having occupied a table near the window, I was taking a series of sips of the hot brown liquid when I looked up casually and saw the plump figure of Portuguese Joe standing at the counter, staring in my direction. As I watched he looked away then started to walk towards me, his eyes fixed on the floor. Just when it seemed that he was going to leave without acknowledging my presence, he stopped beside me. Gazing over my head at the traffic in the street, he placed his hands in the pockets of his off-white linen jacket. For several seconds he stood motionless in this position, then slowly, simultaneously, drew from one pocket a silver-plated lighter, from the other a packet of Greens. The lighter clicked and, still without turning my head, I looked up and caught his eye for a fraction of a second. Smoke streamed from his nostrils as he let out a breath.

'O'Brian's,' he said softly. 'One o'clock.'

Before I could answer, he moved away. I watched him bang into a bus driver who was trying to stabilize several teas on a tray. An apology was muttered but not, judging by the man's expression, gracefully accepted. Portuguese Joe walked quickly out into the street.

It was a short walk from the Ajax Cafe to my offices, which were situated in a converted house on the Ormeau Road. I rented both floors but, owing to a lack of staff, seldom used the upstairs rooms. (At this time I had only one assistant — a small round-shouldered individual called Herman.) On the glass door of my ground-floor office I had painted:

BERNARD HOLLAND & ASSOCIATES.

Sometimes, in the late afternoon, this would be reflected in a magnified form onto the wall nearest the door. I used to enjoy looking at that effect.

After unlocking the door I switched on the fan hanging from the centre of the stucco-decorated ceiling; its blades started grudgingly to move, cutting into the stale air. I hung up my hat on a hook by the door, then crossed to the large wooden desk that dominated the room. I clicked on the desk-lamp — the type that has a flexible metal support enabling the light to shine from any direction. I sank into my leather-upholstered swivel chair, then slowly filled and lit my favourite Peterson pipe, puffing up a haze of fragrant, white Turkish smoke. I switched on the radio; it was Mozart. Beautiful, easy Mozart. I turned off the desk-lamp. Sunlight was streaming through the bamboo blinds in the window, highlighting one of the freshly painted white walls. I was feeling mellow; even the wave of tiredness that swept over me felt pleasurable. My mind was blank and pristine like a baby's.

The door opened and the postman entered breezily. 'What about you, Bernie?' he said, reaching me two inches of mail bundled by an elastic band.

'Oh, just the same, Jackie. The 'Pool going on any tours this summer?'

For a few minutes, as the postman slowly backed away, we discussed Liverpool's prospects for the coming season. I suggested that they had passed their heyday and were now entering an inevitable decline.

'Perhaps you're right,' he said brusquely from the pavement, letting the door swing shut.

Deciding to look at the mail later, I locked it in a desk drawer, then re-lit my pipe. Since I had settled with my long-term creditors several weeks earlier, opening the mail was no longer the uncomfortable, almost harrowing experience that it once was. The wave of dunning letters and phone calls had been reduced to a mere trickle, and I no longer felt uneasy each time the phone rang. Blokes were calling at all hours saying I owed them this and I owed them that. There seemed to be no respite. And although I am fairly resolute in my business dealings, all these ultimatums were seriously affecting my equanimity.

In order to improve the situation I borrowed a book from the library about relaxing and forgetting your troubles, but it seemed to contain nothing but platitudes and time consuming exercises. I tried one exercise designed to produce mental equilibrium by listening to the rhythm of one's breathing. This, however, I found to be more disconcerting than anything else. All that wheezing I was conscious of for the first time made me think that I was in one of the earlier stages of emphysema.

For the next couple of hours I busied myself with the sporadic affairs of my three unlimited companies. Janus Import and Export, Blue Angel Introductions, and the Rapid Results Investigation Agency.

I still hadn't got round to locating that hussy who waltzed off with a client's collection of first-edition Romantic poets a mere two days after I had introduced them. I advised him to go to the police and let their Art Squad worry about it. But he didn't want them troubling his wife when she returned from an extended vacation in Canada. Apparently the woman had been offered the use of his wife's bedroom for a night or two: a kindness she repaid by supplementing her haul with four antique rings and a rather expensive fur coat.

I was so dismayed by this vile act of trickery that I agreed to commence investigations regarding her whereabouts, and although it was against Agency policy to work for nothing I did grant him a thirty per cent discount off the fees.

O'Brian's was big and very solidly built, with a bar that stretched for almost twenty yards. Throughout the pub, wood was the predominant material: oak and mahogany that enhanced the polished brass fittings and mirrors advertising brands of whiskey unavailable for twenty or more years. Every opportunity had been taken by the builders and decorators to adorn with elaborate carvings and designs in wood and plaster. On the wall behind the bar there was a board with rows of small bulbs; pressing a button on the wall of each snug lit the appropriate bulb, which in theory summoned the waiter.

Ensconced in the first snug, I lit one of my nutty, crackling Camels and addressed myself to my pint.

'Bernard.'

A tremor of disquiet passed through me at the sound of this strange, gasping voice. I looked up sharply. Portuguese Joe gazed down at me over the top of the swinging doors; his brown eyes were troubled and his black hair, usually oiled and brushed back in immaculate style, was ruffled. He was breathing heavily.

'Have you been running?' I asked gruffly as he lowered his bulk onto the bench facing me. I looked up anxiously at the door. Portuguese Joe continued to puff and moan.

'Well, have you?'

'Chased by a dog,' he rasped. Beads of perspiration had formed on his large upper lip and his forehead. He dabbed at his face with a monogrammed handkerchief, folding it carefully before replacing it in the pocket of his linen jacket. I noticed that even when distressed he still held his head characteristically to one side.

'Bloody great thing it was, too. Came out of an entry snarling and snapping, went straight for my heels. God knows why it picked on me.'

He lit a cigarette, inhaling deeply; rather than increase his breathlessness it seemed to help him breathe more easily.

'Must have done something on it,' I said, not trying to conceal my pleasure. 'Dogs don't attack without a reason . . . Wasn't rabid was it?'

Moaning, he abruptly started to unlace his left shoe. 'Think it got me here.' He pulled off the sock and examined his heel and the back of his lower leg. 'Can't see anything.'

'Don't worry. There are no reports of rabid dogs in

the province.' I summoned the waiter. 'Now, tell me, what's all this about?'

I waited while he replaced his sock and shoe, combed his hair and dabbed once more at his face.

'Basically, this is in your interest, Bernard,' he said in his usual polished voice, his composure now regained. He seemed to think for a few seconds, then smiled, perhaps at my expression of scepticism. 'Well, yes, my own interest is somewhat involved here also — perhaps that goes without saying. But I want to be completely frank with you, Bernard —'

'Frankness is not, I'm sorry to say, a quality I normally associate with you.'

He looked hurt. 'Oh, come now, we're not still stewing about that little thing, are we? Look, what can I say? *Mea culpa, mea culpa, mea maxima culpa?* There, I've said it. Is that enough or should I get down on my knees?' He started to intone. 'And why beholdest thou the mote —'

'Let's dispense with the theatrics,' I snapped, still annoyed over that episode of the previous summer when Joe sold me a shipment of cigarettes which turned out, to my genuine surprise, to be stolen. What particularly irritated me was the statement he made to the detectives which practically accused me of setting the whole thing up. 'And don't try to suggest that I'm holding umbrage because of some minor incident. You know better than that.'

He nodded, subdued. The waiter entered. Portuguese Joe ordered a dark rum and another pint.

'I'm sorry, Bernard. But it is rather a jungle out there, isn't it?'

'At times. Now, shall we get down to brass tacks?'

'All right.' He lowered his voice. 'Faye Dunslaney is your niece, is she not?' I nodded. 'How well do you know her?'

'Not very well,' I said. 'Her father, Marcus, was my wife's brother. They never got along. We weren't even at his funeral.'

'Her mother's dead also? She was the only child?'

'Yes on both counts.

'That's what I heard. Now, I'm not certain about this but I think that, oh, no more than six months ago her father mailed a letter to himself from the west of Ireland. If my sources are correct, it contains information on certain companies that I'm interested in. It's not terribly important, but I would like you to get it for me.'

I said nothing. The waiter returned with the drinks. Joe paid him, then leant forward and said, almost in a whisper: 'I *am* prepared to pay for it.'

'Naturally you'd pay for it. You'd better tell me more.'

'As I said, look for a letter with a west of Ireland postmark, particularly one from Donegal. If the envelope has been discarded you'll have to tell her what you want: she'll know what's happened to the letter. But try the other way first; think up some pretext for going through his papers — something to do with the family.'

'Why don't you ask for it yourself?'

He sighed. 'Because she'd ask awkward questions, that's why. Questions that it may not be in her interest to ask.'

'I'm sure you're greatly interested in her welfare.'

'Only to the extent that I prefer to get what I want without people getting hurt.'

'And you're not going to tell me what it's really all about?'

'Bernard, believe me,' he smiled, 'it's better that you don't know.'

He lifted his glass, and as he drank his eyes stayed fixed on mine; eyes, subdued only minutes earlier, now confident, expressing hidden knowledge, the power to hurt. I reached for my pack and slowly lit a cigarette and thought of his veiled threat regarding Faye.

'You're not planning to blackmail anyone, are you?'

He shook his head emphatically. 'No. You have my solemn promise on that.'

'I won't be a party to anything like that —'

'I've given you my word, Bernard.'

'All right. So what kind of money are we looking at?'

'Well, considering the special nature of my request, that is, the necessity for you to be, shall we say, less than honest with a member of your own family, I am prepared to be generous. It's probably wildly excessive, but I will pay fifty pounds upon delivery.'

I said nothing for a while. I just stared at him, looking for an indication of what this document was really worth to him. But he returned my gaze evenly, giving nothing away. Finally I said:

'You know, I don't think that's being wildly excessive at all. I think you could quite easily double that figure.'

Again he looked hurt, but this time it wasn't feigned. 'Now, now, old chap. Let's not get carried away. Fifty pounds is more than ample.'

Several minutes later we had agreed on sixty pounds. This, I felt, was quite satisfactory considering that any document I passed to him would not be the one obtained from my niece. I don't like threats, veiled or otherwise, and I don't like people who have made things difficult for me with the police.

He finished his drink and stood up. Then, as if he had been reading my mind, regarded me with a mixture of suspicion and anxiety.

'There's no reason why we shouldn't be able to work together, is there, Bernard?'

'I'll give you a call when I get it,' I said.

We stared at each other for a few moments, then Portuguese Joe nodded and went out through the swinging doors.

As I pondered Portuguese's request, his air of mystery, his threatening undertones, I could not help but be amused. Did he really think that I — a former operative of British Intelligence, not to mention three years' experience running the Rapid Results Investigation Agency — would be so naive that I would do as he asked? Did he think it had escaped my notice that Marcus Dunslaney, a convicted stick-up man, disappeared at the same time a Belfast bank was robbed of close to £150,000? I didn't know if the police had made this connection, but it was strengthened in my mind at least when one month after the robbery he was found in the Atlantic ocean with a bullet hole in his skull.

Chapter 2
A girl has to live

Immediately prior to my occupancy the downstairs office was used as a second-hand clothes shop. On the morning that I took possession of the building I found that the previous tenants had left behind most of their stock. This clothing was in such poor condition that I couldn't sell it as a lot or even give it away; so I dumped it along with the other rubbish they had left and continued with the seemingly major task of cleaning up.

In the basement I was pleased to find some bamboo blinds rolled up in the corner. These will save me some money, I thought; no need to buy those venetian blinds now. And right enough, they looked the correct size and were in such good condition that I, in my too eager acceptance of an economy, did not pause to consider their one serious limitation.

Some nights I would be sitting at my desk, not wanting to go home, reading a novel, having a few drinks — and I would look up to see sections of faces at the window. A gallery of eyes, tips of noses pressed against the pane, moustaches and thin, sneering mouths. Sometimes the more uncouth elements among them would tap on the window and shout insults like 'Drinking the piece out again, Holland?' and 'Reading your case-histories, Sherlock?' So I had to buy a fabric blind on a roller for night-time use.

During the day the bamboo blinds were perfectly satisfactory. Indeed, one feature which I had initially regarded as a defect almost justified my decision to instal them in preference to the venetian type . . . When the blinds were put up it was noticed that they were approximately six inches shorter than the window.

This was not, I thought, a serious shortcoming, and I proceeded to disregard it until one day, when sitting at my desk, listening to the radio and smoking my pipe, I noticed that this gap was, for most women passersby, right about crotch-level — a section of the human form so vastly more attractive than those displayed by the evening riff-raff that by the end of the rush-hour on that particular day I found myself in a state approaching mesmerization.

Business was slow the morning after my meeting with Portuguese Joe, but I wasn't looking through the window; my mind was on the problem of my domestic situation and, in particular, a curious incident that had occurred that morning.

Usually I left for the office before my wife got up — we slept in separate rooms — and on entering the bathroom at the usual time I noticed that the light was on. Thinking that it had been left on all night, I got out my razor and brush and was building up a good lather when in she came wearing nothing but her briefs. (God help her wit if she thought she was tormenting me with the inaccessibility of that body.) 'I'm still in here,' she said loudly, avoiding my disdainful look. Then, seeing me shake my head — an expression of contempt for this pettiness more than an indication of refusal — she gave me a push, hitting the small of my back against the washstand. And so, before this morning incubus of blazing eyes and bouncing breasts, I proceeded to back out, my arrival in the hall barely preceding the slamming of the bathroom door.

Reflecting later on this nasty little incident, I was amused to recall the erection that was evident as I completed my shave in the kitchen, a form of tumescence that I had long since ceased to associate with my wife.

But, pondering my domestic vicissitudes was by no means the most appropriate application of my time this particular morning, so I settled my attention on the problem of approaching Faye Dunslaney. Not exactly, as Holmes used to say, a two pipe problem, but it was in fact two pipes and two mugs of tea later before I concluded that the best approach was along the lines suggested by Portuguese Joe, that is, the pretence of being on family business. I dialled her number.

'Faye? . . . This is Bernard Holland here. Remember me?'

'Yes.'

'Good. How's everything with you?'

'All right.'

'Good. Look, there's a little matter here that's just come to my attention. May I call round and talk to you about it?'

'What matter?'

'Well, I'd prefer to talk to you in person about it. Let's just say that it could be to your advantage.'

'I'm just going out, but I might have time later on. If so, I'll call at your office.'

'The address is —'

'I know where it is.'

Not, I thought after hanging up, the friendliest of people. She had made me feel as if I were trying to inveigle her into one of those pyramid-selling schemes. Perhaps this haughtiness was inherited from her father. Marcus always struck me as being somewhat of a cold fish, too serious by half. I never could get along with him, even during recent years when we were both in our own ways estranged from his sister.

I switched on the radio. Prokofieff, I decided after some consideration. Good stuff, no doubt, but a little too gloomy for my taste. I switched it off, then settled down to some serious work. Faye put in an appearance shortly before 4:30.

Almost disdainfully, she strolled around the downstairs office, looked behind the beige curtain that covered the cracks in one wall, then, after kicking the brown leather couch, glanced down as if expecting to see an exodus of scurrying insects.

I said: 'To my knowledge, only one person has ever hid behind that curtain. I found her one evening, naked and cowering and half out of her mind. My partner was responsible for that.

'He's no longer with me,' I added.

She came over to the desk. 'I heard about him.'

Dale Diamond used to handle most of the investigations. After he was gunned down on a case two years earlier I worked relentlessly to find his killer. It was my tip that led to an arrest. (That episode will, I am confident, form one of the highlights of my autobiography, provisionally entitled *Case-Histories of a Soldier-Detective*.)

I had remembered Faye as an attractive girl: now I was gazing at a very beautiful woman. If anything, her incivility on the phone and now here in the office placed her beauty in a sharper relief, increasing her desirability. It seemed from the way she walked and looked at me that she was very conscious of her loveliness, expecting, as a tribute to it, acquiescence from every man who entered her aura.

And as I sat there enclosed within, as it were, the inner circle of that aura, I found myself in a state of mind that can only be described as one of uneasy awe. Never before had I been in the presence of a glamorous green-eyed black-haired woman: a rare form of female which I, in my romantic intoxication, associated at that moment with adventure stories and daring heists of jewels. My mind flashed with images of besotted desperadoes hung up by the feet by bandits; of Russian roulettes with blood-tipped hands and fully-loaded revolvers; of electric-shock handshakes, and husbands breaking down doors with axes, and cops getting out of cars.

Having, apparently, already rejected the leather couch and having dismissed with a glance the two armless hard-backed chairs, it seemed no more than appropriate when, pushing my stoneware mug to one side, she established herself on my desk (an executive area strictly out of bounds to that infinitely less exalted form of creation, *Homunculus Hermanicus*), sitting directly upon my file of Janus correspondence: a positioning, I thought, entirely wasted on the non-sentient faces of that ancient Italian god. The aptness of her familiarity was further enhanced when, leaning back with her hands behind her on the desk, she proceeded slowly to cross her legs, exposing to an almost zenithal degree an expanse of black nylon.

Glancing up in response to a noise which had presumably originated somewhere in her throat, I was immediately aware of the unlit cigarette held between two backward tilting fingers and pointing provocatively in my direction: an attitude struck, so it seemed, not only to reproach me for my lack of attention to her requirements but also to indicate the idea that under appropriate circumstances possibilities might just exist over and above the pleasure I had derived from looking at her thighs.

After I extended my lighter, she inhaled deeply and then, over a diagonal distance of about three feet, responded to my courtesy, albeit an unpunctual one, by blowing the faded grey smoke gently over my face. Whether this was an expression of her displeasure or an unusual way to tantalise a prospective intimate, I was undecided; at any rate, after my initial surprise I did, with some misgiving, allow her a certain amount of credit for having done it gently. Then, with no thought of retaliation — though the pungent Turkish and American tobaccos would have been particularly effective — I reached for my pack of Camels.

'I always thought Uncle Bernard was quite well-off,' she said, glancing pointedly around the room.

'Don't be deceived by appearances.'

She flicked ash into the stoneware mug. 'Meaning?'

I did not, in fact, know what I meant. It was just something I said to give the impression that I was not, as she seemed to think, down on my luck, As I saw it, I could refuse to expand on my intimation, one, it must be admitted, not likely to make much dint against the patent reality of my circumstances, or I could use it as a basis for redeeming a situation that had clearly deteriorated within the past two minutes.

'As a matter of fact, this present state of disrepair is intentional.' I paused to collect my thoughts. 'It is intentional because I am presently liquidating all my assets. And that' — the inspiration was sudden — 'is why I need your help. I am leaving my wife.'

Having said it and having, I felt, reacted to my own

statement with a much greater degree of surprise than was evident in her own barely changing facial expression, I found the words gushing out in an almost cathartic manner.

'Yes. Just about had enough of that woman. Made my life a misery for far too long. No need to bother you with all this, though. Just thought I'd explain why you're here. I've decided —'

'Before we get into all that, do you think I could have a drink? I'm absolutely parched.'

'But of course. Bad manners on my part not to have offered you one earlier.' I stood up. 'I've got —'

'If you've any beer, that will do.'

Returning with two bottles of Black Label, it came as no surprise at all to find her sitting in my chair, though I was a little taken back by the sight of her swivelling from one side to the other with an almost childish pleasure.

'I like chairs like that,' she said, getting up and going over to the couch.

'It's a good one, isn't it? My assistant, Herman, can't wait till he gets me out so he can sit there and pretend he's some big noise.'

I poured out the beers, carried them over to the couch, then sat down beside her. 'You see, it's these papers concerning my wife. Apparently, they were sent to your father earlier in the year. . . .'

I think at that point, imagining her to have mellowed somewhat, I had formed a distinctly erroneous idea regarding the facility involved in obtaining permission to examine her father's papers. Her attitude became so intransigent that not only had I, in order to justify my proposal, to entangle myself in a large web of lies — progressively becoming more absurd and embarrassingly intimate — but I was forced to offer her a sum of money considerably larger than the almost nominal amount I had contemplated as a token of my appreciation for her trouble — the bestowal of which, I had imagined, to be accompanied on my part by an avuncular smile and, in the face of her blushing reluctance to accept, a steadfast insistence that my generous impulse should not be thwarted.

I should have known better. I should have remembered that the only time I had ever dealt with a beautiful woman with black hair and it hadn't cost me money was back in '60 when I held open a door for an ex-beauty queen. Still, I would have preferred that the consideration required to secure Faye's compliance had been even a trifle less than the fee agreed upon with Portuguese Joe.

After she left — the arrangement was that I would go to her house the next morning — I felt sufficiently inspired by our encounter to resume work on a long short story called 'The Nyloned Foot' which I had been dabbling with for some time.

(As yet, only one of my literary efforts had seen publication. This was a poem titled 'The Prisoner' which appeared in a fairly prominent Irish literary journal. When I tried to repeat that success by submitting another poem, I was informed, quite curtly, by the editor that no further contributions from myself would be welcomed. Apparently, a Dublin schoolmaster had written a letter claiming that 'The Prisoner' was a rank plagiarism of one of James Joyce's poems. I replied with relish that if the editor would re-read my published poem as carefully as he should have done in the first place he would notice a rather scurrilous acrostic containing at least one word not current in James Joyce's day. Needless to say, that revelation served only to reinforce the ban on my writings; but I considered my trick to be well worth the loss of a literary outlet, and a fairly stuffy one at that.)

After putting in a good hour on the story — I revised the section regarding an unintentional kick caused by a burning cigarette end falling onto the unshod foot — I was interrupted by the appearance of an unusually crestfallen Herman.

'Got thrown out again, have we?'

'Aw, now.' In his peculiar sloping gait he went over to the couch and sat with his head in his hands.

'A drink make you feel any better? You can have some of my Old Comber.'

He shook his head; then, as if suddenly realising what he had refused, got up and crossed directly to the filing cabinet where I hid my booze. I suppressed an impulse to ask him how he knew where the whiskey was kept.

'So what's the problem?'

'It's something personal.'

'And what am I? A stranger you just met in the street?'

He stood at the cabinet, looking pensive. I didn't know whether he was debating the appropriateness of confiding in me or whether he was wondering if he could get away with another drink.

'Have another. *In vino veritas.*'

'I saw Frieda,' he said dully.

Frieda, mountainous and goodnatured, used to be his girlfriend; and like himself, she had not — to put it not too unkindly — found herself near the front of the line when the Almighty made that all-important issue of cerebral matter; indeed, after noting her remarkable tolerance of Herman's antics, I sometimes wondered if she had been present at all, having been perhaps mistakenly herded, in company with the genuinely bovine elements of creation, towards a different allocation point altogether. Nevertheless, while their affair lasted it had a distinctly beneficial effect on Herman.

'I'm a person now,' he told me, with tears in his eyes, on the evening of their first date. And in the weeks that followed he developed a new confidence; he became talkative and, for the first time since I had known him, told ribald jokes, and laughed with the knowingness of an initiate when I related my own spicy stories. In particular, it used to delight him when, with a look of feigned envy, I would wink and call him 'old ramrod'.

But, as I foretold, it was only a matter of time before Herman started to take outrageous advantage of her passive nature. After a year of anguish and embarrassment, she changed her address without telling him.

Herman grieved for almost six months. At first he would spend long hours sitting morosely in the basement; then, apparently taking a dislike to being indoors, he would spend each day wandering around the city, his head bowed. (In order not to let all this walking go to waste I did, in fact, equip him with two sandwich boards advertising my latest line in surgical equipment.)

Although I tried my best to comfort him, it didn't seem to have much effect: it was doubtful, I felt at the time, if he even understood what I was saying. He was, to all appearances, a mute animal, badly hurt, unable to rationalize what had happened, and lacking a philosophy with which to comfort himself. Still, there was no denying the healing power of time and in the end Herman came to terms with his loss, if not himself.

But now, a year later, was it really possible that this Frieda business had not, after all, been laid to rest?

'What did she say?'

'Nothing. Didn't say nothing. Turned her head away.'

'But you told me you'd got over her. Didn't you say that?'

'It was true when I said it.'

'Herman, I'm not sure I could put up with you if you start to carry on like you did before. There is a limit, you know.'

I tidied my papers and placed them in one of the drawers; then I turned the beam of the desk lamp against the wall and sat back with my pipe. Herman was on the couch, his head slumped over his knees; and as I looked at him in the subdued light — his rounded back, his child-sized legs, the strands of brown hair fallen away from their position above the bald area — I felt for a moment immensely sorry for him.

'I'm still trying to fix you up with someone from the dating agency, don't forget.'

'You said that before.'

'Look, you're a member of staff here, and by rights I shouldn't consider you at all. God, think what those newspaper sods would make of that. Agency staff using lonely women for their own pleasure . . . Herman, you don't know what those people are like. Look how they made a big thing of that redhead. I didn't know she was asking for money. Had my suspicions, mind you. But the thing was, nobody ever complained about her.'

'I fancy that redhead.'

'Well, she hasn't come back yet but when she does I'm going to ask her point-blank. I won't put a tooth in it. Was she or was she not using my agency to sell her fanny.'

'How much you think she costs?'

'What's that? You getting ideas in that direction now?'

'I only asked.'

'Believe me, Herman, it wouldn't be worth it. No, you just hold on and I'll dig up something for you. As good as Frieda anyway. I've always believed in looking after my people — you know that, don't you?'

'Can I have some more of your whiskey?'

'I said look after, not spoil. Don't you have any of your beers left?'

'I thought there was two left but I must have drunk them.'

'Oh, all right, have some more, but you're going to get yourself into a state if you keep on thinking about Frieda. Drink and bad thoughts don't mix, you know.'

Shaking his head, he went over to the cabinet, poured and drank a small one, then poured another, which he carried over to the window. For a while he stood there, holding back the blind, almost motionless, just looking out.

'Bern.'

'What?'

'You remember the last time, when you said I was thinking too much about her and you made up those scenes that I could think about when I couldn't sleep?'

'You mean the Fearless Shadow, the Japanese Warrior — that type of thing?'

'Well, I did think about them. I liked them. But my favourite was the man who could do everything. What's he called again?'

'That's Renaissance Man. You want to do him tonight?'

'He's better than Mystery Man.'

'All right. Come over here and I'll go through it again . . . It starts off when you're taking a blonde out for a spin in your new plane, and you decide to land at Cambridge to see your old professor. As you stroll into the laboratory you notice that everybody is upset because they can't solve a very important problem. You, of course, take in at a glance what the solution is. "Why don't you try this?" you casually remark, stepping up to the blackboard. And as you give your explanation the boffins keep snapping their fingers and muttering "But of course, of course." So you have to tell them to keep the noise down because you're due to play in the Cup Final that afternoon and there's no time to lose.'

'Why don't you try this?' Herman repeated, taking up a position before an imaginary blackboard. He doodled in the air for a few seconds then slewed round, a fierce expression on his face.

'Keep the bloody noise down, you dummies.' Then, jumping up and down like a monkey, his features twisted almost out of recognition: 'I — am — not — going — to — tell — you — again.'

'That's the ticket. That's exactly how it should be done.'

'Can we do the Unknown Hero, too? The one where —'

'Not tonight, Herman. I'm tired and it's getting late. I want to close up now.'

As I locked the office door Herman stood at the top of the stairs leading to the basement where he lived. 'You never know,' he said, 'some day I might make a discovery.'

'A scientific one, you mean?'

'Maybe. Maybe not.'

'Goodnight, Herman.'

As I walked to the sidestreet where I kept my '63 Zodiac, I tried to organise in my mind the events of the day; but owing to fatigue I found myself superimposing them to such an extent that by the time I reached the car my only recollection of the past twelve hours was an image of a black-legged Faye, cigarette in mouth, bamboo cane swishing at her side, directing into an ominous-looking laboratory a reluctant party comprising my snarling, topless wife, a mooing Frieda and a two-faced, chittering Herman.

Chapter 3

Episode at the Albert Clock

Faye's living room was decorated in what I would call a Californian theme. Although I have never visited that part of the world I have tended to associate its interior design with an air of soft-hued simplicity, uncomplicated but not unsophisticated, achieved by clean lines, light matt colours, and the skilful juxtaposition of artifact and natural article.

It was this last aspect that immediately caught my attention as I followed her into the spacious room. Three of the house plants — two areca ferns and one other I couldn't identify — reached almost to the ceiling; an effect that was striking but not incongruous or dominating. Three red-flowered plants were positioned along the diagonal of the wall-set, enhancing the array of leather-bound books and china figurines. All of the woodwork — the door, the coffee table, the cabinet, the wall-set, the legs of the fawn-coloured couch and chairs — seemed to have been fashioned from the same type of blond wood. The fitted carpet was light fawn, almost white; the reason no doubt why I had been asked to remove my shoes.

Faye, wearing a black robe with a green oriental dragon design, approached the cabinet. 'Care for a drink?'

'Please. Anything at all.'

I tossed an envelope containing the money onto the coffee table. As I did so, this action, like a jolt or a small particle precipitating a state of crystallization in a supersaturated solution, brought into focus the tantalizing feeling I had experienced that there was something suggestive about these surroundings, notwithstanding the fact that, from my viewpoint at least, there was no aspect of this house that could be termed, without unduly exerting the imagination, disorderly. The idea of Faye — the use of a short robe satisfying the requirements of both display and convenience — lolling about as one of the least solicitous elements of a Western *tableau vivant,* her insouciance deriving from the security afforded by the allegiance of a spasmodically captive market, induced in me quite a forceful snigger, which I was not able to completely suppress.

'Something funny?'

'Oh, no.' I accepted a glass of sherry. 'I was just thinking of something my assistant said this morning. Nothing to do with you.'

At this she gave me a fairly sharp look, which caused me to realise my mistake. 'No, I didn't mean it wasn't any of your business. I meant that the joke wasn't about you.'

'Don't worry about it. Sit down.'

She pointed to a chair and then sat down on the couch facing it. She lit a cigarette, depositing the spent match in a green Connemara marble ashtray. I reached for my pack of Camels.

As the seconds passed and the silence threatened to become uncomfortable, I searched for something to say. 'Hope I'm not putting you to any great trouble,' I offered.

'Actually, I've just got up. I'm not feeling so hot . . . We'll have a drink or two, okay?'

I smiled and nodded. What that really meant, I decided after a few moments' reflection, was that, possibly owing to a not uncommon disinclination to make conversational efforts directly after rising or, as was hinted, the possession of a 'head', she wanted me to keep the noise down; an injunction which Herman — who, as I noticed earlier that morning, was becoming increasingly enraged by the still-muttering boffins — would have been delighted to deliver on her behalf.

Not in the least put out by this apparent taciturnity — I did in fact welcome the opportunity for indulging in undisturbed admiration of her reclining form and, to a much lesser degree, the nonchalance she was displaying by drinking alcohol after she had, by her own admission, just got out of bed — I relaxed in my chair and began to sip contentedly at my sherry.

Then, in a manner similar to that of yesterday, she increased the scope and intensity of my approval by performing — no other word will suffice — a movement that, apart from its fundamental mechanics, bore in its execution so little resemblance to the corresponding motion mundanely carried out by the general body of mankind that to refer to it simply as crossing the legs would be an understatement comparable with that of designating Handel's *Messiah* as a piece of singing.

'You've got beautiful thighs,' I said.

Amusement, perhaps pleasure, flickered in her eyes. 'I like a man who's open about what he likes. Not many would have stared so long' — she started to laugh — 'or so obviously. Good for you Bernie.'

I began to chuckle too, although — having hoped for a slightly less condescending response — I wasn't aware that the situation was all that funny. Still, allowances have to be made, I thought, for the feminine sense of humour, especially one stimulated by the unimpeded circulation of one or two pre-mensal glasses of sherry.

'Well, sitting around like this isn't getting us anywhere, is it?' she said smiling. 'I'm sure you're a terribly busy man. All these assets and whatnot that need liquidating. Much too complex for me, that sort of thing. I'm afraid I'd find myself right out at sea.'

'I don't know about that,' I said, taken back by her choice of metaphor, 'but it can get quite tricky at times.'

'I'm sure it can... Anyway, I've been going through his papers and I've put the important-looking ones in that cabinet over there, right at the bottom. So have a look there first. If you can't find it, then I'll have another search upstairs.'

The Dunslaney Papers — as I had somewhat facetiously come to think of them — were not, as it turned out, a collection which merited much interest at all. I had been under the impression that my payment to Faye was made in order to compensate her for any embarrassment, or even risk, to which she might have been subject; however, I was now beginning to think that it was simply a matter of rank opportunism on her part. It seemed that the only thing I was paying for was, for all practical purposes, her suspension of disbelief regarding my somewhat questionable reason for examining the papers in the first place. The only documents that at the conclusion of my audit I felt promising were two letters and a sheet containing columns of figures.

I went over to where she was sitting. 'Where did these come from?'

She studied them for a while, then said: 'These letters were from Dublin. This other one I don't understand. He sent it to himself. It arrived not long after he . . . well, disappeared.'

'Did you throw out the envelope?'

'Yes, but I did look at the postmark. A place called Dunglow, in Donegal. I even looked it up on the map.'

And so, it appeared, I had turned up something after all. I had another glass of sherry then told her I had to leave. As she reached me my hat in the hall I said:

'We'll meet again, I hope.'

'All right,' she said and opened the door.

I nodded goodbye, then went out into the sunlight and walked down the path to my car.

The one aspect of my wife's post-honeymoon behaviour that placed the most strain on our already tenuous nuptial bond was her seemingly automatic refusal to believe a word I said. This policy of hers — and that, I believe, was just what it was — may have been employed to attack my equanimity, or even my sanity, but its effect on me was no more than a feeling of intense irritation. Consider this exchange:

'So we're sleeping out now, are we? Took up with the fancy woman again, have we?'

'I spent the night in the police barracks.'

'Like hell you did!'

'I was accused of receiving a quantity of stolen cigarettes.'

'You bloody liar! Stolen cigarettes! What kind of a gull do you take me for? I know where you've been.'

'Quite a large quantity, in fact.'

'In fact! In fact! You don't know what the word means. You're a bloody Walter Mitty, that's what you are. Big time bloody fence indeed!'

So you can imagine the sneering incredulity, the laughing in my face, when I had on occasions referred to my wartime stint in British Intelligence. Even with my pals down at the pub my assertions in that direction were almost invariably met with a sardonic smile and a facetious attempt to humour me — and occasionally, in the case of less sophisticated types, a fairly obvious nudging with elbows. Yet, annoyed as I might have been at this treatment, I was never in a position to pull out a pay book and retort: 'See here. What does this say?' In my day at least, operatives were not as a general rule issued with identification.

All this tended to be quite exasperating, so I used to find particularly gratifying those occasions on which I was able to utilize one or more of the skills accumulated during my years 'underground'. And when, in Faye's living room, I had noticed that the figures on that sheet of paper were arranged in groups of five (grouping is a standard procedure to disguise the length of 'words'), a small surge of excitement was felt, and I envisaged the possibility of once more being 'in the field'.

Dunslaney's cipher was quite simple, almost childish in fact. The letters of the alphabet were arranged in jumbled order to form a square which was numbered one to five vertically and horizontally (since there were only twenty-five places in the square, I and J were doubled up). Then each letter of the words in the message was represented by its two numerical co-ordinates.

I should say that, scornful as I was of Dunslaney's naivety in choosing such an elementary cipher, I was relieved he had not used one similar to the simple but unbreakable cipher I invented during the war. (I use the verb 'invent' in the sense that I was unaware of its existence elsewhere at the time that I developed it; however, its simplicity was such that it was conceived, on an independent basis, by other intelligence agencies. What I found to be particularly rankling was the refusal, without explanation, by British Intelligence to adopt my cipher. And in light of the fact that several of their ciphers and codes were indeed broken by the Axis agencies, I think that I can say — albeit with the benefit of retrospection — that a little less haste in the rejection of my ideas may well have been appropriate. I shall have much more to say on this matter in *Case-Histories of a Soldier-Detective*.)

Any cipher that repeats itself, that is, uses the same figure each time to represent a letter, can be broken using frequency tables. My idea was to encode in the normal way then add a random number to each group and transmit the total. The random numbers are arrived at by opening a pre-named ordinary book at random and turning the words into their figure equivalents. The page and starting line are simply tagged on to the message so that the receiver can determine and then subtract the random numbers.

But that's enough technical talk. (Incidentally, an undercover character I developed for Herman during his difficult spell — the Unknown Hero who swept fear into the hearts of the Nazis when he sailed from Ardglass in a fishing boat and decoyed their battleships to their doom — met with on his part almost complete indifference. A lack of response which, considering the potential contained in such a character, I found quite surprising; indeed, especially so when contrasted to his rackety enthusiasm for the Japanese Warrior. The Samurai being of course a tradition completely alien to the Western mentality, which, however inappropriate the term may seem, must be regarded as sufficiently comprehensive to permit inclusion of Herman's intellectual processes.)

The deciphered document gave, as I had expected, a position relative to certain landmarks, and I felt it logical to assume that an item of value had been buried or otherwise concealed at that location. However, since no place names were given, it was not possible to determine what district or even what country the location was in. Certainly I had one clue: the town from which the letter had been posted; but I could not be certain that the position referred to in the document was in the vicinity of Dunglow; and even if it were, I realised that I could spend months covering the area and still not locate the landmarks, and all the while making myself thoroughly conspicuous. What made matters worse, in that it ruled out the use of ordnance survey maps, was that some of the points of reference were individual trees.

I was pondering these difficulties when the front door opened abruptly; indeed, had the door not offered resistance in the form of a self-closing mechanism, the force applied to it would have been sufficient to propel it violently against the wall. It was obvious from Herman's expression as he passed by me at a fair clip on his way to the back room that the courtesies normally extended to one's employer after an unauthorized absence of several hours would on this occasion be dispensed with on the grounds that they would be excessively time-consuming.

Again the door was opened, and this time with such vigour that, the self-closing mechanism notwithstanding, there was a resounding crunch as the handle dug itself into the plastered wall: a feat of strength I would have admired, even applauded, had it taken place on any other premises but my own.

'Do you realise that wall has just been painted?' I enquired somewhat rhetorically of a stocky individual in jeans and a white tee shirt who was looking around the room in a distinctly menacing fashion.

Then, as I watched with a mixture of irritation and fascination, he embarked on a wild-eyed examination, punctuated by grunts and accusatory glances in my direction, of every possible place of concealment in the room; some of which, the top of the filing cabinet for instance, could not possibly, even allowing for Herman's diminutive stature, have been utilized as a place of refuge. Then, as if sublimating the physical and emotional momentum of his search into a glare that seemed in its intensity the very epitome of grievance, he regarded me from under the unbuttoned peak of his cap and said, apparently without opening his mouth:

'Where is he?'

Now, although still unaware of the nature of my assistant's misdemeanour, I felt this interloper's attitude was one that very definitely precluded any possibility of co-operation on my part in delivering to him or even producing for interrogation the small fugitive who, if not exactly cowering in the back room, was at least, quite sensibly, remaining completely silent.

'I'm not having this,' I said firmly.

Although it hadn't seemed possible, he now managed to impart to his glare a new, almost inhuman intensity. '*You're* not having this?'

'You're danged right I'm not. I don't know what's going on here, but I've had all I can take of you . . . Come on, out you go,' I added, raising my voice and waving once or twice in the direction of the door as if ordering out an unruly or muddy dog which, contrary to instructions, had found its way into the house.

He stood his ground. 'I want that wee man.'

'You're not having him.'

It was at this point, as we were staring aggressively at each other, the administration of blows (as opposed to their exchange) being, on my part at least, not only contemplated but planned, that the situation was somewhat defused by the appearance of a customer. Apparently disconcerted by this development, the stocky man cast a baleful glance at the passage leading to the back room — to enter which it would have been necessary for him to pass within three feet of the sides of my desk, a manoeuvre I was determined would not be successfully executed — looked around the office again, as if seeking some object on which to vent his inarticulate rage, then turned on his heels and stamped out.

No sooner had he done so, there was a sudden movement past my desk and Herman was in the middle of the room, jumping up and down and shouting, 'You dummy! You dummy!'

'Herman! Control yourself.' I turned to the customer, who, quite understandably, was showing signs of increasing discomfort. 'Don't worry, he doesn't mean you. A little tensed up, that's all.'

The customer nodded, then watched anxiously as the subdued Herman padded his way towards the front door.

'Where do you think you're going?'

He stopped, but didn't move or speak.

'Don't you think you would be better off not going outside for a while? Besides, you're probably anxious to explain a little matter to me, aren't you?'

He sat down on the couch, and I returned to my business transaction. Five minutes later the customer left.

'Now, what was all that about?'

Herman's brown eyes regarded me dolefully for an instant, then returned to their examination of his paint-covered fingers.

'Well, he was sitting on our window sill eating fish and chips . . .'

'Yes?'

'So I told him that wasn't allowed and he kicked me.'

'What happened after you told him it wasn't allowed and before he kicked you?'

'Well, his fish and chips got knocked over.'

'What you mean is, you knocked them out of his hands, right?'

'Something like that.'

Sighing, I reached for my makings; then, slowly filling and lighting my pipe, I considered how, given a lack of communication, minor hostilities have so often developed into major ones and, in particular, how excessive zeal on my assistant's part has so often embroiled me with people of all ages and from all walks of life, united only in their passionate desire to administer to him a severe beating.

'Herman, I have a lot of work to do, and I don't want you here in case that man comes back. Here's a pound. Off you go and be back here for six o'clock. I want you to take a letter to Portuguese Joe this evening.'

'Six o'clock, Bern.'

'Yes, and in future keep your nose out of other people's business. Be sensible.'

'I'll be like the Japanese Warrior, Bern. Just watching and thinking and watching and —'

'Yes, yes, you've got it. Now clear off.'

I made a mug of strong instant coffee, stirred in a teaspoonful of clover honey, and brought it out to my desk. As I saw it, the crux of the matter was obtaining more information about this document without revealing to Portuguese Joe that I was becoming further involved. Caution was necessary here, for there could be no doubt that P.J. remained, in the words of my former associate, Sid, 'a very nasty piece of work indeed'.

But, on the other hand, it was also true that in the face of determined opposition Portuguese Joe would almost invariably back off; he would do so with dignity, even apologies, but at the same time vowing to bring about his opponent's downfall as completely and painfully as he could. (I know for a fact that it was Portuguese Joe who started those rumours that were current shortly after the business with the stolen cigarettes; the aim being of course to damage my credibility by making me a laughing-stock of the pubs. But how anyone could believe that in 1944 Joe's father saw me home on leave wearing an Aussie hat, two first world war medals, and carrying a U.S. Army kitbag, I just don't know.)

Furthermore, it was, I thought, almost certain that Portuguese Joe had me at a fairly serious disadvantage: he knew, presumably, what he was doing. I did not. Before I could grab a bewildered Herman and shout 'Come, Watson, the game's afoot; bring your revolver' (Heaven forbid Herman with a revolver), I needed to be enlightened regarding the exact nature of the game. When it came down to it, all I had were rumours and a document that was, without further vital information, quite worthless to me.

Anyway, I resolved to play it by ear, and set to work producing a new coded document for Portuguese Joe. I retained as much of the original as possible, the only basic difference being of course that the co-ordinate landmarks were changed.

Having missed lunch, I was feeling a little hungry by this time, so I locked up and went down to the local cafe. Shortly after 5:30 I returned to my desk and, somewhat lethargically, resumed my ponderings on the whereabouts of the shapely book-snatcher.

As I reviewed the hypothetical steps that one would take to dispose of the stolen valuables, I really must have dozed off because the next thing I knew I was sitting in the dark. I rubbed the stiffness out of my neck and then looked at my watch. It was 11:15. I made myself comfortable again and watched as a passing car's headlights flashed obliquely through the bamboo blinds, running their distorted image along the white wall.

Then more headlights flashed and a chill went through me as the grotesque shadow of a man played on the wall. Instinctively I dropped to the floor. My head was clear now. No point in being quiet, I thought grimly: he knows where I am. With one sharp movement I opened the bottom drawer and brought out my old army knife. Then, holding it with the blade in front of me, I crouched like a spring in preparation for the attack.

'What's the matter, Bern? It's me.'

It was Herman. I got to my feet.

'I've just been mugged,' he said.

I stared at his dark motionless figure for a long ten seconds, then:

'You nearly got your throat cut, you realise that, don't you? Why the hell did you sneak up on me like that?' I was, needless to say, fairly angry.

He limped up to the desk and stood there, breathing heavily; there was a strong smell of alcohol on his breath. He looked distraught; his shirt was torn. He threw up his hands and said loudly:

'Honest, Bern, I was mugged. Look at my shirt. I wouldn't lie to you. I was mugged.' Then, pausing as if remembering something, his hand went to his neck. 'And this' — his voice faltered — 'this is gone.'

Apparently he had lost his small gold charm, an object which he considered to have protective, almost magical, properties.

'Okay, sit down. Where did this happen?'

'At the Albert Clock.'

'Did you tell the police?'

'No, I just wanted to get away. There was three of

them. They knocked me down and kicked me. I didn't even see what they looked like.'

A car horn sounded loudly, making him start. Although not conscious of it at the time, I recalled hearing the same noise while I was reaching for my knife.

'Oh, I forgot. I took a taxi. As I was running away I saw one. I told him to wait.'

'Meaning I have to pay for it, uh?'

He nodded glumly. I glared at him, then went outside.

'How much?'

The cabbie, a thickset man with a boxer's nose, regarded me with animosity. 'Three pounds,' he said sourly.

'Three pounds from the Albert Clock to here?' It seemed excessive.

'Three pounds,' he repeated in a peremptory tone. I saw his hand close on an object resting between the seats; it was a tyre-iron.

I shrugged and paid him. Squabbles with taxi drivers, I thought, would have to wait for more settled times.

Herman was sitting just as I had left him. He didn't speak as I slowly cleaned, filled and lit my pipe. I switched on the desk lamp; the light, in a clearly defined beam, shone down onto the top of the desk. I relaxed in my chair and through the large cloud of smoke hanging over the desk, slowly curling and rising in the beam, Herman and I regarded each other, his dark brown eyes unwaveringly fixed on mine as if trying to gauge my mood or impress me with his apparent candour. Irritated though I was, his baleful expression almost caused me to smile.

'Well, you probably need a drink after your ordeal,' I said.

Grinning broadly, he rose and went over to the filing

cabinet.

'Bring a glass for me too.'

He grimaced as the whiskey went down. 'Arrgh, that's good, very good.' Not being, for basic economic reasons, omni-bibulous, he usually confined himself to beer and tended to gulp all drinks, including spirits.

'Do you know what I would love right now?' he said, grinning.

'What, Herman?'

'A smoke of one of your pipes.'

Herman had learned to smoke pipes before I knew him; and, reluctant to purchase them himself — an understandable attitude in one whose pipes were frequently left behind in pubs — seemed to regard it as his right, an element of his remuneration almost, to claim my discarded pipes; a practice which, owing to my fear that he would drunkenly set fire to the building, I was not at pains to encourage; and consequently, when he did in fact successfully claim one of my superseded Petersons or Careys I was always glad when he did lose it. On this occasion, however, it seemed appropriate to withhold objections.

'All right.' A search of my desk drawers revealed an old smoked-out briar. 'Here you are. Help yourself to the tobacco.'

Once it was lit, he sat back contentedly, his eyes half-closed. 'Oh, I love this pipe. This is . . . mmmh . . . lovely. It's so . . . mmmh . . . lovely.' He looked up dreamily. 'I must have this pipe . . . mmmh . . .'

With the aid of two simple pleasures — a glass or two of whiskey and a pipe — he had passed in the space of a few minutes from apparent trauma to a state that can only be described as one of serenity. Although not entirely unexpected by myself, this Micawber-like transition still struck me as being remarkably abrupt. My plan, conceived while paying off the taxi, had been to discontinue direct interrogation and thus promote in him a state of relaxation, from which, it was hoped, a smattering of truth would emerge. However, as it turned out, he was apparently so enraptured by the pleasures of smoking that no information of any description was to be volunteered.

'Herman, if I had been out when you got here tonight, how would you have paid the taxi?'

He grinned. 'I was lucky you were.'

'How much did you lose?'

'Nothing. I didn't have no money.'

'And you're sure you didn't see what these blokes looked like?'

For a few moments he seemed to be re-living the episode at the Albert Clock: his eyes went out of focus, his features were strained.

'They weren't all blokes, Bern,' he said slowly. 'One of them was a woman.'

Chapter 4

Bedrabbled, bothered and bewildered

Reading hard-boiled detective stories I am often amazed by how much action a private eye can see in such a short period of time. After getting coshed once or twice, escaping from a sinking car or two, outwitting killer dogs, being betrayed by his well-stacked female confidant and, during the quieter moments, tangling with the local cops, he finally exposes the drug-dealing politician or saves the small seaside burg from the mob: and all this seems to happen in three or four drink-sodden days.

Well, after the events that followed my encounter with Portuguese Joe that Monday morning, I was starting to think that those stories were not so farfetched after all. So when the three days following

Herman's experience with the muggers turned out to be almost entirely uneventful, even on the domestic front, it was with a feeling of considerable relief, tinged perhaps with uneasy expectation of further disturbances, that I seized the opportunity to eliminate the backlog that had developed in my ordinary business affairs.

As I had expected, Herman was unable to recall further details pertaining to the attack. When asked if he had informed anyone that he was supposed to deliver a document to Joe that evening, he vigorously denied it. As to why he did not return to do just that, he said he 'fell in with some blokes and forgot': a reason he also advanced to explain his presence in the vicinity of the Albert Clock, a location considerably distant from his normal stamping grounds.

I delivered the document to Portuguese Joe myself, meeting him in O'Brian's and concluding the transaction as quickly as possible. When, in an ingenuous fashion, I wondered aloud why he should show such keen interest in a list of figures, he said, straightfaced, almost solemnly: 'Bernard, I can now disclose to you the precise nature of these figures. They represent, in numerical form, the identity of certain shares which, by a method known in the trade as the the boiler-house tactic, will be temporarily raised to an extremely inflated value. I need not elaborate on the opportunity presented by such knowledge.' It would have been difficult at that point, I thought, to determine which of us was directing the most laughter up our individual sleeves.

On Saturday afternoon, alone in the office, I came to a decision concerning Herman. I had for some time felt the need for a person to adequately replace Dale Diamond, and although Herman did not make great demands on the budget, his usefulness was, to say the least, open to question. Indeed, my mounting resentment at his unreliability and outlandish antics had earlier that afternoon taken a decidedly physical expression: a form of chastisement which, I now realise, was both richly deserved and long overdue.

Returning from a pub luncheon, only slightly effusive as a result of my host's generous dispensation of Old Comber whiskey, I decided to demonstrate the efficacy of my recently acquired false beard and nose by entering the office unannounced and in the guise of a commercial traveller engaging Herman in conversation regarding the whereabouts of his employer.

I had hoped prior to entering that Herman was not, contrary to instructions, sitting at my desk; and, in a sense, it could be said that he was not; although, considering the infinitely more reprehensible position in which I discovered him, that was definitely no cause for self-congratulation on his part. He was, in fact, slumped over the desk.

As I repeatedly cleared my throat and drummed my fingers on the top of the filing cabinet, his head slowly rose and two glazed eyes looked dimly into mine; his mouth opened and closed then opened again and finally:

'Holland's Investimegations . . . May he help you?'

I suppose that three years' experience of this man's misconduct should have prepared me for this moment; but as I stood there, gazing down at my prostrate assistant, his bald patch shining under the lamp, I was both very angry and very disappointed. But this was not all: Fate had one more shock in store for me; and as I pondered the immensity of this man's most outrageous dereliction of duty, my eyes perceived but my mind did not believe. Even Herman, I thought, could not be so foolhardy, so presumptuous: it was out of the question. I reached over and removed it from his grasp, his arm twitched then lay still. I held it, warm in my hand, and realised that it would never mean the same to me again.

Yes, it was so: he had been smoking my favourite Peterson.

Slowly, the head rose once more; he looked at me for a few seconds with an expression that seemed to demand an immediate explanation of why my not altogether desirable person was to be found in his office; then, apparently exasperated by my trance-like condition, he said in a drawn-out aggressive slur:

'Well?'

It was at this moment that I lost control. I can vaguely recall rushing at him, lifting him up by the front of his shirt and swearing wildly into his face. After that I must have heaved him over the desk and dumped him on the floor. At this point I regained my presence of mind: I remember cautioning myself to take it easy before I seriously hurt him: but even so, I was still not satisfied. I pulled out one of my imported canes from behind the filing cabinet and started to lay into him with that, swishing him across the legs as he danced and howled up and down the room. Then, after we had been around the office twice, I threw down the cane and went out to my car to cool down.

The office was empty when I returned to it fifteen minutes later, having removed the beard and nose and put on another jacket. Well over an hour passed before Herman decided to venture back. He at once proceeded to explain his absence: '. . . Like a maniac, he was, Bern. Had a big beard and awful eyes . . .'

I should add at this point that this new hard-line I was developing towards Herman did not necessarily involve his expulsion from the office basement, where he slept. I had no wish at all to render him homeless, to force him out onto hostile streets where, unable to shift for himself, he would rapidly develop into a minor thief and wino. No, it was simply a matter of confining him to janitorial duties and re-grading his former position of factotum so that it could be filled by a person of considerably more executive ability.

Therefore, with this as one factor and a greatly increased scope for obtaining information regarding her father as another, I decided to offer the position to Faye Dunslaney. And, of course, just having her around was a pleasant enough prospect, adding an element of class to the premises, even if, as I had quickly discovered, she did tend to be a little abrasive.

There was no reply when I attempted to phone her around six o'clock, so, resolving to try again later, I settled down with a coffee and the bulky historical novel I had been reading in the more leisurely days of the previous week. However, it soon became apparent that the plight of the young naval lieutenant immured under sentence of death in a brutal Spanish prison was now, in contrast to my former interest in his sufferings and the *modus operandi* of his inevitable escape, a matter of complete indifference to me.

Not sufficiently in the mood for working on my autobiography, I decided to turn my attention to my other work-in-progress, a collection of long short stories with which I had been occupying myself in an intermittent fashion for the past four years. Currently working on the third one, I required just two more stories to complete the volume.

'The Nyloned Foot'. ('A grateful public will thank Mr Holland for this almost definitive treatise on foot fetishism.')

'Two Strange Women Sitting on a Yellow Table'. ('Mr Holland explores with exquisite wit and understanding the formerly unpublicized mystique of the *derrière*.') (This story, inspired by one of Grimm's tales, relates the downfall of a petty official who comes into possession of a wishing table that will magically provide all that his heart desires.)

'Troglodyte on Tenterhooks'. ('A milestone in the investigation of sensory deprivation . . . this highly literate work is both entertaining and thought-provoking . . .')

('To say that the publication of *Case-Histories of a Soldier-Detective* has caused a stir in Parliament would be the understatement of the century.') ('It can now be revealed that the newly-formed Intelligence Police, acting on Sir Bernard's instructions, have rounded up all Marxists and closed the L.S.E. and B.B.C.2 . . . he also issued a stiff warning to trade-unionists, students, immigrants, "progressive" church-leaders, local governments and the unemployed.')

Not the best way to spend Saturday night, I suppose, but what can you do when you're between girlfriends? What with concentrating on this Dunslaney case and clearing up backlogs — not to mention Herman's carryingson — I had neglected to make arrangements to provide for such a contingency. In my dissatisfied state, even that redheaded tramp from the agency was being regarded in a distinctly more favourable light.

I tried once more to phone Faye. Then, for no particular reason except that I was feeling restless, I decided to take a walk in the direction of her house.

As I strolled down the Lisburn Rd I saw my old enemy Mrs O'Harnessey approaching.

'Not on the drink tonight, Mrs O'Harnessey?' I asked politely.

It was a cheap shot, I knew; but she really was a formidable drinker and was occasionally to be found at my office window mouthing unintelligible insults. As a boozy nuisance she was, according to my experience of that class, to be rated only slightly below Herman. On this occasion, however, she was, as I had perceived from her gait, quite sober and did not respond to my loaded inquiry.

'Not on the batter tonight, Mrs O'Harnessey?' I shouted for good measure. 'Not on the barge tonight, Mrs Batter? Not on the tear, Mrs Adair?'

'Got a light?' said a woman stepping out from a chemist's doorway on the corner.

'I have, indeed.' As I held the match to her kingsized I noticed that she was blonde and strikingly attractive in a brash sort of way. 'Haven't I seen you down at the concerts?' I asked, just to be saying something.

'Don't think so.'

'No? Could have sworn I saw you at the Mozart do last month. I thought you were behind that young chap who tipped out of his seat during the pianissimo. He'd definitely been drinking.'

'I don't care for concerts.'

'Not everybody does. You live around here?'

She laughed. 'A policeman wouldn't ask you that.'

'Don't get me wrong, I'm not being forward. I just thought that we could walk together if you're going in my direction. It's getting dark and the way things are in this city at the present time. . . .'

'No, really.'

'The other night an employee of mine was viciously attacked. He was in a terrible state when he got back.'

She thought this over for a few seconds. 'Well, you may be right . . . You live in this area, don't you? I think I've seen you before.'

'You probably have. I have premises on the Ormeau Road. Fairly well known around here, in fact.'

After we had walked a little way she turned and said: 'Don't get the idea . . . well, I just thought what you said made sense.'

'But of course.' I nodded knowingly and fell into step.

We arrived at her house and I was not at all surprised when she asked me in for a drink. It was, she said, the least she could do. That sounded promising, but I appeared somewhat reluctant. 'Oh, that's not necessary.'

'Come on,' she said, taking my arm.

I sat down on the large couch in her nicely appointed though nondescript living room and lit a cigarette.

'Scotch okay?'

'Fine.'

She placed the bottle on the coffee table and as she sat down beside me her skirt rode up her thighs; she gave it a perfunctory sweep of her hand and it stayed where it was. (I had already noted the high quality of her thighs: one has certain preferences even when confronted with an array of localised attractions; and fortunately, assuming a large degree of co-operation or, at least, sufferance on the woman's part, the choice is one of precedence rather than exclusivity.)

We continued to make small talk and it was not long before my hand, descending from a contrived gesticulation, found itself languishing on her knee: a contact which, in pace with the momentum of the conversation and animated by the implications of her extreme and self-determined proximity, became progressively more enterprising until the point was reached where my hand had disappeared beneath her skirt.

Curiously, neither by word, glance nor gesture did she respond to this premature familiarity: her complete attention seemed to focus on ensuring that the level in my glass did not fall below the half-way mark, and all the while speculating in a perfectly affable manner on the weather conditions to be experienced later that night and the following day. Indeed, such was my disconcertment resulting from her absolute lack of recognition of my embassy, directed, by the nature of things, towards the majestic court, that I even contemplated withdrawing my hand until such time as the situation could be placed in its proper perspective. However, being an old soldier and consequently a believer in the maxim, Take what you get and say nothing, I decided to press home my advantage and commence the divestment of her person.

Leaning forward to permit the removal of her blouse, she remarked on the likelihood of approaching rain. I agreed and drew her towards me; she smiled; then, just as our lips touched, there was a clicking sound and for a moment the room was brilliantly illuminated. Catching sight of a man as he ran out into the hall, I started to rise, then felt the blonde's hand on my arm.

'Let him go. It's only my husband.' She shook her head dismissively. 'I've told him off before about doing that. Popping out from nowhere when I've got company and flashing that silly camera. It's so embarrassing.'

I started to get up again, found myself staggering, took a few steps like an elderly bent man to correct that, then, using the wall for support, rose to adopt a more dignified posture.

'I'd better go now,' I said. She just shrugged. I shook my head, feeling a spasm of deep regret. I lifted my hat and walked out.

It was pouring. I stepped quickly but carefully down the gently flowing street. I put my collar up, pulled down my hat, and some rain ran into my mouth. I was a fool. Once more into the jaws of the honey trap charged the old agent. Without an overcoat. In the direction of the wrong guns charged the soldier-detective. After he'd heard two weather reports forecasting rain. Pursue the bitch until she catches you. In shoes that were now starting to let in.

I trudged down the Lisburn Rd for a few minutes then stopped under a ledge to light a Camel. There was a man and a woman about fifty yards down the street. I watched as he put his arm round her; she wriggled away, ran a few steps then seemed to deliver a kick to a shop door. She ran to the next shop front, and this time there was no doubt at all regarding her intention. Stepping back to the edge of the footpath, she ran at the door and a loud crack could be heard as her foot connected with it.

After she had administered the same treatment to two more doors, the man crossed the road and climbed into a sports car. He sat there for a little while, revving the engine, apparently waiting for the woman. She was now standing at the kerb, looking in his direction as if deciding whether or not to go with him.

By this time I had moved up and was close enough to make out her features. She had looked like Faye from a distance, but apart from her figure and her long black hair there was little resemblance. She was quite young and was wearing a black coat that ended, just below her knees, in a thick fur turn-up.

I said hello. For a few seconds she didn't move; then she slowly turned her head and looked at me.

I have been in my time the recipient of many vicious looks, but in terms of sheer malignity the expression in this young woman's eyes will always be remembered as being in a class of its own. As I turned away I suddenly felt older and wetter and shabbier. My tired legs moved in heavy steps along the streets that would lead me back to my office and the bottle of Old Comber.

It was after midnight when, singing sadly to the bright moon, I walked, on footpath and on road, the short journey home. I just want to go to bed, I thought as I tried to key the door, and wake up the next day but one.

The wife played hell the next morning. 'Tell your father,' she shouted at Bernadette, our daughter, 'that if he ever comes in here again drunk and falling down stairs . . .'

I just walked out and left her to it. Poor Bernadette, getting the old suffering wife routine again. I did, in fact, mention to the wife that her behaviour was the real reason our daughter seldom visited us, but the campaign was too advanced for her to consider or even understand issues like that. In other words, her resentment was all-consuming, pervading, or so it seemed, even the physical structure of the house: antagonistic doors that banged my head; windows that refused to open; sore points laid throughout like mines, waiting for me, tripping me on the stairs.

I could still hear her shouting as I went along the path to the gate: 'And I had to go and marry a man who has no sense of responsibility whatsoever . . .' I felt like going back in there and telling her that if I had no sense of responsibility I would have walked out on her long ago, but I just shrugged and went on.

I phoned Faye from a kiosk and she said to call round but to give her half an hour. It was sunny and I had a little time to kill so I decided to set out on foot.

She made me a cup of tea, then I started to outline my proposition, looking at her all the while to catch a look or expression that would reveal her thoughts. But she remained impassive, sitting in a blue dress on the couch, applying mascara, tilting her head back and looking in a small handmirror. I was beginning to doubt that she was even listening.

'Well, what do you think?'

'I'm not sure.' She went over with her makeup to the wall unit, lit a cigarette and stood with her back to the shelves, her Egyptian eyes staring across the room. 'I'm not sure about this commission business.'

'The point about being on commission is that there's no limit to your earnings —'

'It's the lower limit I'm thinking of.'

'That's negative thinking. Give it a month, see how

things shape up. You'll be surprised at the potential of my new schemes. At least one of them's going to hit the jackpot; absolutely bound to.'

After a few seconds she said: 'Oh, I suppose I can give it a try . . . but I can't start until Thursday.'

'That's all right. It'll give me — or Herman, I should say — time to spruce up the offices. He'll have them shining.'

I had another cup of tea while she painted her nails, then she said she had to get ready to go out. That seemed strange because she was already made-up and dressed to the nines and I wondered where she was going on a Sunday afternoon in Belfast, looking like that, wearing a short blue dress and a necklace, her hair shining and fragrant with conditioner, and with a black beauty spot painted on her cheek.

But I didn't pursue the matter. My interest in her was now composed of so many incongruous elements — uncle, detective, admirer, employer — that my hangover couldn't cope with it.

Chapter 5

Under fire on three fronts

On Monday morning, after rousing Herman and setting him to work painting the exterior woodwork, I made a list of his other chores to be completed before Thursday, which included cleaning the brown carpet in the downstairs office and polishing the wooden floor of the upstairs one. I also made a mental note to watch out for him taking all day on any one job. Herman would be, on occasion, possessed by a mania for what he conceived as perfection, often spending enormous amounts of time on quite a simple task, fussing and changing and changing back, and invariably making a complete balls of the whole thing.

At approximately 10:30, I was sitting at my desk when the door opened and a man stepped in. He was of medium height, stocky, wearing heavy-framed glasses and had a rugged, clean-shaven face. He glanced round the office for a few seconds then pulled his hat down over his eyes and strode up to the desk.

'You Bernard Holland?' he snarled.

'Yes, me Bernard Holland,' I snarled back. There may have been a certain resemblance between us but I still didn't like the look of him.

'And make it short,' I added. 'You're wasting private time.'

He grunted and a small revolver appeared in his hand. It was a nice trick, but I'd seen it before. I heard him growl 'Goodbye, sucker,' and as the gun roared I was moving to my left. Two more quick shots seemed to come from his blurred, almost dancing figure as I went for him, fast and swerving. Then, like a crack, it came into focus and I put everything I had into one short blow.

For a moment after his head hit the wall he remained standing; his eyes were wide open, staring but blind; his hand went out and hung in the air as if wanting to shake hands; then his head sagged forward and he crumpled to the floor.

Now that it was over I felt so shaky I had to lean against the desk. I was gulping for air and my heart was thumping wildly. Resisting the impulse to run out of the office, I knelt over him and went through his pockets, glancing up at the door every few seconds in case he hadn't come alone. There didn't appear to be any identification: just keys and money. I went over to the door and opened it cautiously.

It didn't seem as if any of the people on the street had noticed anything; at least, there was nobody gawking or pointing in my direction. I couldn't see Herman. I closed the door behind me and started to walk. Pausing in a doorway I lit a cigarette with trembling hands, trying hard to fight down the feeling that everybody was looking at me. Then I started to walk again. I wasn't going anywhere but I needed time to figure out what to do next.

It's a question of noise, I thought. The police will land in on me only if somebody heard the shots, and the sound of a lightweight revolver indoors on a busy street might well have gone unnoticed. Thinking along those lines put me in a better frame of mind; and as I walked from the Ormeau Bridge back towards the office I was feeling quite cheerful, blithely expecting to find that the gunman had picked himself up and departed suitably chastened, and Herman merrily painting away at the front.

Indeed, the more I thought about the incident the more I admired what I had done, even indulging myself to the extent of a swagger or two and, once or twice, pushing idling pedestrians out of my way. After all, I thought, becoming more intoxicated by the second, they hadn't tackled empty-handed a desperate armed gangster; they were just humdrum people going about their humdrum business, whereas I was on a dangerous mission, under attack from blondes and bank robbers and the henchmen of Portuguese Joe.

Even the sight of the patrol car outside my building did not dampen my spirits. The car was unmarked but there was no mistaking the almost tangible aura of policeness that seemed to surround it. I strolled into my office. There were two policemen going through my desk.

'Ah, Sergeant Murkley,' I said, as if savouring a rare and unexpected delight. 'It's so gratifying to contemplate the eagerness which you display in maintaining our acquaintanceship.'

'I'll do the talking, Holland,' he snapped, moving away from the desk.

Murkley was big, with a large raw face. His partner was young with red hair, and standing with his pad poised he looked apprehensive as if this were his first outing in plain clothes.

'What happened to Dolan?' Murkley said.

'Who's Dolan?'

'The man we carried out of here.'

I sat down in my chair. 'Listen. A very ugly customer came into this office today, pointed a revolver in my direction and pulled the trigger several times. Under those circumstances I thought it prudent to defend myself. Did I do wrong, Sergeant?'

Murkley bristled. Placing his foot on one of the visitors' chairs he leaned over the desk and regarded me severely for several seconds. Then his mouth opened, exposing the top row of a set of shining false teeth, and there was a slight rattling sound just before he shouted:

'Holland, you're in serious trouble.'

We all have our favourite stories about the unexpected ejection of dentures. Who hasn't known at least one person to drunkenly spew his top plate out of a train window or into a toilet that was then flushed? And although expulsions caused by shouts are probably, apart from drink-related cases, the most common category, I had never until that moment witnessed one that achieved such a spectacular range.

'Good God,' mumbled the sergeant, looking down in wide-eyed surprise. Then, pulling out his handkerchief, he scooped them up and shot me an accusatory glance as if I had been responsible, by some sleight of hand, for their appearance there. After restoring them to his mouth, he proceeded with his accusations regarding Dolan.

It was, of course, a ludicrous situation: being berated by a pompous sergeant of police immediately after his teeth had bounced twice in front of one and barely missed landing in the ashtray. There was, under the circumstances, just no possibility that I could respond soberly to this talk about 'complaints' and 'information from certain sources' or even contemplate the mire of 'serious trouble' which, as the sergeant liked to explain in his hackneyed graphic terms, was ever threatening to envelop me.

'. . . And I know for a fact that Dolan . . . Look, Holland, I'd seriously advise you not to find this funny.'

'Sergeant Murkley,' I said, smiling broadly, 'why don't you give me a chance to tell you what happened?'

He sat down on one of the visitors' chairs and gave a long sigh. 'All right, Holland, let's have your version.' I told him the story; the rookie took it down.

'Why didn't you report it?' asked Murkley. 'You know bloody well all incidents involving firearms have to be reported.'

Suddenly I got a little mad. 'Maybe I didn't call the police because I thought it wasn't necessary. Maybe it was because I was too busy trying to stay alive. Or maybe it was because I had two broken wrists.' I reached for my pack of Camels. 'Besides, Herman is under standing orders to report all shootings in this office.'

'Don't talk rot.' Murkley lit one of his small filters and tossed the spent match in the general direction of the ashtray. 'So you and Dolan were in it together, eh?'

'In what, for godsakes?'

'Dolan came out of prison yesterday. He served five years for a payroll job. The money was never recovered. First thing he does is call on you with a loaded gun. So I'm wondering, what happened? You blew his share, that it?'

'You're a great talker, Sergeant.'

'Okay, Holland, play it cagey. But it won't do you any good.' He glared at me for a few moments, then: 'What are you working on now?'

'Well, there was this tart with a taste for poetry, furs and antique rings —'

'You know what I mean! You're working with

Portuguese Joe again.'

I wheeled back in my chair a little and lifted my feet onto the desk. The remains of the hangover from Saturday night was wandering about inside my head. I closed my eyes.

'Sergeant, I'm suffering from too much booze, too little sex, and too many irrelevant questions. If you want me to talk some more about Dolan, we'll do it down at the barracks.'

'Aye, it'll be different down there, all right,' said Sgt. Murkley, just before the door slammed.

I can recall being in an Army recruiting office in 1940 at a time when the corporal was asking a young man if he had a criminal record. After a good deal of hemming and hawing the young man finally admitted that, yes, he had once been arrested for housebreaking. When was that? he was asked. After going through the facial expressions associated with racking one's brains, the potential recruit stated that he couldn't remember. 'Can't remember?' exclaimed the amused corporal. 'I think if I was arrested for housebreaking I'd remember it all right. That's what I would call a red letter day.'

I don't know what became of the corporal but I believe that if I related to him the events of that Monday the words 'red letter day' would immediately spring to his lips and he would congratulate me on surviving an attempt on my life, laugh with me at the little farce played out with Sergeant Murkley, and nod his agreement with my handling of the threatening phone call . . .

Shortly after lunch a muffled male voice stated that he had a photograph of me *in flagrante delicto* (embracing the blonde with great thighs) and unless I stayed away from Miss Dunslaney this evidence of my extra-marital excursions would find itself with great speed in the hands of my wife. My reply was a request that he do just that — she deserved a good stiff jolt — and could I have a copy for my album? He didn't know what to say.

It was of course a serious mistake on his part to confirm the link between the Dunslaney document and the blonde; and if she hadn't decamped after her sordid little entrapment, that constituted a lead which I intended to pursue without delay. Furthermore, it was now clear that more information could be obtained from within Faye's house or from Faye herself.

As I pondered the phone call and its implications, it became evident to me that I had seriously underestimated the progress I had made on the case. There was just no other explanation for the frame-up and the visit by Dolan. Somebody out there was getting nervous. And indeed, when I recalled tough clever cautious Dale Diamond being carried out of a dirty side street with two bullets in his chest, I felt more than a little apprehensive myself.

At four o'clock I locked up the offices and shouted for Herman. Having decided to implement a policy of tight security, I wanted to be sure he was present and correct (i.e. sober) to keep an eye on the building.

There was no response. I descended into the basement — trying not to breathe in too deeply — but he wasn't there. Slacking off as usual, I thought bitterly. Well, he may be in for an unpleasant surprise when Faye takes over as his supervisor. Unless I'm a Chinaman, she'll put the clamps on him all right. Then it'll be time for the grinding of teeth and yearning for the good old days under the Bernard regime.

And if he complains to me, well, I'll just say 'As you are now classified as a disruptive element it behooves you to co-operate with steps being taken to ensure your eventual rehabilitation.' That won't mean anything to him of course but it will establish the new tone. And if Miss Dunslaney is not there when I say it, then I'll repeat it when she is, preferably while seated at my desk, my hands held steeple-like before me, cufflinks gleaming, and wearing my Intelligence Corps tie over a freshly laundered white cotton shirt.

It was coming up to the rush-hour as I eased my car out into the traffic and I was glad when I reached the quiet streets of the blonde's neighbourhood. As I went past her house I noticed a black Austin saloon in the driveway. That had not been there on Saturday night. I drove around the block then parked several doors down from her house. I settled down to wait.

In my erratic career as a private detective and proprietor of Rapid Results Investigations I have done a lot of waiting: slumped down in the seat of my car, standing in the rain and, on one or two occasions, waiting for hours to go into court. Giving evidence in those matrimonial disputes was a little trickier than it might appear; particularly after Sergeant Murkley brought up, quite maliciously, a certain technicality prohibiting those with police records becoming private detectives.

(I use the term 'police record', rather than 'criminal record', to emphasise the reasonable doubt that existed with regard to my role in that wretched affair which Murkley used as the basis for his objection. I still maintain that I was entirely unaware that those paintings the Professor kept at my place were forgeries. And when I did start to suspect that something was wrong I found myself faced with a dilemma regarding the poor old art director who had, believing them to be genuine, bought them. I knew that if it were all brought out into the open he would be in trouble and so, basically on his account, I kept quiet. Then I was arrested. How the Professor got away I still don't know. I'm still looking for him though; him and that female-gangster wife of his, called Billie.)

At any rate, that is why I can never admit to the police that I, personally, am working on a case. I think that people in cushy government jobs who come out with all these petty regulations would find it illuminating to enter into the real world and find out for themselves what it is like to be an independent businessman. How many of them, I wonder, could wait, with no guarantee of remuneration, for five hours in a car outside a blonde's house?

Yes, it was dark when I drove away from there and during that time, apart from the living room lights coming on, there had been no sign of movement. I was tired and thirsty and my throat was raw after smoking almost a pack of cigarettes. A dismal end, I thought, to my first red letter day in ages.

Chapter 6

The Sailor hits bottom

The next day I made myself scarce. Not available for comment. Not available to photographers, police, wives, gunmen, or gawkers. I spent most of the time sitting in my car outside the blonde's house — seven hours of almost unrelieved boredom — and by mid-afternoon I found myself dozing off. (Having decided to give home a miss for a few days, I had spent the previous night sleeping fitfully on the office couch.)

But I did find out one thing: the blonde was still there. She emerged shortly after two o'clock and drove off in the Austin. I followed her to a supermarket, where she shopped for half an hour, then returned to the house. That was the highlight of the day. I'll give it a few more hours tomorrow, I decided as I drove away, and then that's it: I'm going in.

The light was on in the ground-floor office. Looking through the blinds I saw Herman sitting in my chair, swivelling about dreamily, a bottle of beer in his hand. He got up pretty sharply when I went in.

'Nice to know you come around now and again, Herman,' I shouted. 'Maybe on your next guest appearance you'll finish that bloody painting!'

He was now scuttling towards the back room.

'Stay where you are!'

He came to a halt and turned. 'Honest, Bern,' he began anxiously, 'I was painting yesterday and these blokes pushed me into a car. They took me away and —'

'I'm in no mood for your fantastic excuses.'

'Look, they made me —'

'Shut up!'

I went over to the filing cabinet, poured a very big Old Comber and downed half of it in one fiery gulp.

'We *have* excelled ourselves this past week, haven't we, Herman? I mean, two major incidents in four or five days. A mugging and now a kidnapping. What have we got lined up for tomorrow, Herman? A burial alive? Or is that too ordinary? How about creatures from outer space coming down and taking you to their planet? Would you consider that one, eh?' In spite of my annoyance I had to smile. 'Christ, heaven help their opinion of mankind if they took you for a specimen.'

I gulped some more whiskey, coughed a little, then gave a roar of laughter at the thought of Herman being worked over in some alien laboratory. 'You'd be lucky to get a drink up there, my boy.'

Herman told me this story: He was taken away by big men in dark glasses and moustaches. They forced his face onto the car seat so that he couldn't tell where he was going. They placed him in a dark room and threatened to torture him with a blow-torch if he didn't disclose what I had found out. He thought it prudent to tell them something but knowing nothing about the case, he had to invent a tale about me being after a gang of bank robbers. They kept him overnight then dumped him by the lough, with a warning to keep his mouth shut. The penalty for revealing all this to me would be a horrible death.

I said: 'That's what the French call a *récit abracadabrant.*'

'A what?'

'An extraordinary yarn.'

He looked blank. I don't think he even understood the translation. 'Keep quiet for a minute,' I told him, 'till I think this one out.'

It would be dangerous at this point, I thought, to regard his tale as merely an elaborate excuse for not finishing the painting. If he had been abducted, then the crucial issue was the story he gave to his capturers regarding my activities. In the event that he had been taken by the bank robbers themselves, such a story would almost inevitably prompt them to intensify their campaign against me. (I was assuming here a connection between the bank robbery and the Dunslaney document.) I could not of course attach any blame to Herman — he had merely told them the first tale to enter his head — but I regarded it as a stroke of bad luck that he had thought of one so close to the truth.

The other aspect of his adventure that concerned me was the risk he was taking in disclosing all this to me. If they had indeed threatened him with extinction it was clear that I had done him an injustice earlier by shouting at him. Feeling slightly repentant, I told Herman to get his glass and the bottle of Old Comber.

In the sense that there is no consciousness of unreality, having a dream is like being in another world or universe;

and when that is disturbed and then destroyed by some external means the awakening sleeper often regards, however irrationally, the offending noise or shake as unwelcome, alien or even, in extreme cases, cosmocidal.

Thus, the resentment I directed towards the ringing telephone that awakened me can easily be imagined when one considers the nature of my dream and the fact that not only are dreams greatly superior, regarding awareness or intensity of involvement, to mental images produced in the conscious state but that they cannot, as in the case of images, be conjured up at will.

To find oneself transported from a position, assumed just moments earlier and only as a result of extensive preliminaries, behind a suspender-belted Faye Dunslaney, whose breasts one is kneading and whose crotch is being firmly stroked and prodded by one's priapic member, to a couch in a noisy smoky office is not, in my opinion, the best possible start to one's day.

I remained still until the noise stopped, by which time I was sufficiently awake to be conscious of a sore throat and headache. It was 9:20 a.m. I stumbled out in my underpants to the back room and made some tea.

The phone rang again, and by this time I felt myself capable of answering it. I trudged back, picked it up and said my number. A young man expressed interest in custom-made restraints. Remembering that I would be out for most of the day, I told him to call round tomorrow. Then, from the top of the basement stairs, I summoned my assistant.

'Herman! Herman! Get your horrible little body up here. *Tout de suite.*'

Herman dragged himself up. 'I'm going out now,' I said, 'and I won't be back for hours — oh, not that blue shirt again. You've worn it every day for weeks.'

'I'll be painting, won't I?'

'Yes, I very much hope you will be. But leave that

for now. Do it between twelve and two, and leave the phone off the hook while you're doing it. I don't want you tramping in here and getting paint on everything. For the rest of the time stay in the front office. Put on that suit I gave you and tell everyone who calls that we're renovating but it'll be business as usual tomorrow. Don't say anything more than that. Look intelligent, stick a pipe in your mouth — preferably unlit — and be polite. Got all that? Okay, see you later.'

I picked up my hat and went out to the car. I was feeling a little apprehensive about leaving him there on his own. I felt sure that even if he had listened to my instructions he would either forget them or think about them a few times, thus garbling them until they were unrecognisable — the same sort of thing as soldiers passing messages by word of mouth along a trench.

However, I felt it was necessary to follow up on this blonde without delay. The way I saw it, there wasn't a minute to lose; time was running out, and I wasn't about to let a good lead slip through my fingers because a few shifty-eyed losers wanted oddball items and dates they hadn't the gumption to acquire for themselves in the normal way.

Yes, that's how I thought about what I was doing. It was a cheap business all right — though not as cheap as some people made out — and I felt that it was a severe come-down from my heyday of the forties and fifties, when anything less than a fiver was tipping money, when women stepped forward and men stepped back and they all said 'I've heard about you.'

So that's why I was concentrating on the Dunslaney case; it was my best call to action in ten or fifteen years and I knew that an opportunity like that has to be seized quickly before it disappears.

Two doors from the blonde's house I pulled up and cut the engine. The black Austin was still there and I thought it would do no harm to get organised and check its registration. A postman strolled by and his tuneless whistling seemed to linger in the air. He didn't notice me and he didn't have anything for the blonde. All I had for her was a bad fright, and I was saving that for later. I pulled my hat down to shield my eyes from the sun, then I lit a Camel and started to wait.

By 11:30 I was feeling a little hungry so I unwrapped a chunk of cheese I had remembered to bring with me and nibbled away at that. But it didn't taste all that good so I took a couple of slugs from my hip flask to clear my mouth and as I was replacing the cap I saw a man with a ginger beard walking towards the car. He was large, over six feet tall, and had the rolling gait of a boxer. Even from a distance I knew I had seen him before, and as he came nearer I watched him carefully and tried to remember. Then he turned up the path to the house and the blonde let him in.

At that moment I knew who he was. A few years back when he was in the Merchant Navy, he used to bring dope ashore, pushing it to the rock bands. Although I had no interest in that, I came up against him once or twice when he made advances to a girlfriend I had at the time, Gloria Diamond. (There were times when Dale gave me that sardonic smile of his and I felt sure he knew I was seeing his wife. But nothing was ever said. Dale wasn't the type of man to have double standards.)

The sailor came out and I let him go for fifty yards, then I locked the car and set out after him, crossing to the other side of the street. After a while I could see he was heading in the direction of downtown. He was walking confidently at a fast pace, not looking back.

Within fifteen minutes we were approaching the city centre; the streets were much more crowded with pedestrians, so I moved up closer until I was so near I could have touched him. Abruptly he turned and ran up the steps leading to a tall Government building. I went on past then turned and followed him in. I had been in there before, registering companies, and I knew I would have to stay with him because there were two exits: the front and one leading to a carpark at the rear.

I was not able to determine exactly what type of business the sailor was conducting in that building, but whatever it was it involved a lot of travel from one floor to another and also a lot of waiting. The problem I had in tailing him was that he knew me from the old days and if, as appeared likely, he was involved in the case he would recognise me immediately if I moved in too close. So in order to eliminate this danger I decided to use my disguises.

One minute I might be standing in false beard and raincoat, reading a noticeboard, and the next, brushing the floors in a janitor's coat I'd found and a cloth cap; indeed, for almost half an hour, flashing my mail-order detective badge as a pass, I had to pose as an inspector, pulling out files and asking vague questions, after I had followed him into an area prohibited to the public.

It may seem that going to those lengths was overdoing it a little, and to a certain extent that is true; however, I had carried those hairpieces around with me for some time with the intention of testing them in an operational situation, particularly one like this which involved an extensive period of close following. Moreover, detective work is often so dull that there are times when a little diversion is justified.

There are some people — usually young men — who have the wrong idea about this line of business. They seem to think that it's just a matter of setting yourself up as a detective or even a shyster lawyer and before you can say Philip Marlowe there's a piece sashaying in from the waiting room just as you're buying yourself a short one from the office bottle and although she's got a figure to beat the band her eyes are shy and only slightly sinful, like two kisses in a cathedral, but after you've lit your pipe and wisecracked for a while and heard about her little sister who went out for a manicure and finished up in Mexico, you know she's a cold man-eating broad who figures you for a fall-guy.

But, as I have said, detective work is usually boring. A little less so, perhaps, in a city like Belfast where you're asking questions of supersensitive people who possess more guns and explosives than you could shake a stick at.

Around 2:30 the sailor left with a parcel under his arm. I kept close to him until we reached the Albert Clock then I let the gap widen. It looked like he was heading towards the harbour. I paused to light a cigarette, checking once more to see if *I* were being followed, but if I had a tail he was giving nothing away.

Five minutes later we were in the heart of dockland. I was keeping well back at this point because of the lack of pedestrians, and I think that if I hadn't had the wider range of vision gained from following on the other side of the street I would have lost him after he turned a corner and crossed a side street to enter a small pub with a dirty grey facade and the name painted in brown above the door: Doxy's Tavern. That was all; no Guinness or Harp or Black Label signs to catch the eye; just the name.

Of course, when you ran a bar that was a well-known whore dive you might not welcome customers who hadn't known that buying and selling drink was not the only trade conducted there. And what an ugly lot of baggage they were too. Not that I frequented the place, but on the few occasions I had been there I noted a distinct lack of glamour on the part of the 'girls'.

I gave the sailor exactly one minute then I went in.

Doxy's didn't have big electricity bills but after I'd sat down at the bar and bought a beer — at double the normal price — my eyes became accustomed to the dimness and I began, almost furtively, to look around.

A redhead with big breasts was leaning over a piano; she caught my eye for an instant before I looked away. Three workmen were standing at the end of the bar, talking and laughing. A middle-aged man in a suit sat next to a juke box, looking out of the corner of his eye at a short plump brunette at the next table. Frank Sinatra was singing 'I'll Never Smile Again'.

'That's a great sound,' the man said to the tart. He had a Free State accent. She didn't answer. I still couldn't see the sailor. I sipped my beer and waited. The redhead didn't come over. There was a door marked PRIVATE and as I looked at it through my fingers it opened. The sailor came in and I turned my head away, then I heard his steps moving towards the back of the pub. When I looked round again he was nowhere to be seen.

'He live here?' I asked the barman.

He fixed me with a stare then nodded slightly as if begrudging the information or the effort required to convey it. I tried a long shot.

'Gloria upstairs?'

It was hard to tell, but I think he may have nodded again. He wiped the top of the bar then moved away and started to unload a crate of beer. When his back was turned I went quickly through the door marked PRIVATE and walked upstairs.

I went along the landing to a door. I listened outside for a few seconds then I opened it quietly. She didn't look up at first, and I just stood silently, watching her as she sat on the edge of the bed, brushing her long black hair. I said:

'I used to like doing that.'

She jerked round. 'Oh, Bernie, it's you,' she said. Then she jumped up and kissed me.

As we sat on the bed I asked: 'You and the sailor shacked up together?'

She nodded, then laughed as if the idea were incredulous. 'After you and I —' she began, then broke off as we heard the clump of steps coming up the stairs. I don't know if it was bravado on her part or just contempt for the sailor, but she didn't seem at all concerned as he marched into the room to be confronted with the sight of his girlfriend in a black transparent slip sitting in the close company of his old rival and nemesis, Bernard Holland.

His face was a picture. He didn't know what to think or what to say. He thought he was dreaming. Finally he managed to bang a few words together:

'You bastard, Holland. What the hell are you doing here?'

'What the hell does it look like?' I replied, getting to my feet.

The sailor's right cross would probably have rung up a high score on one of those fairground machines, and if I had stood still and waited for a couple of seconds it would probably have made a mess of my nose or cheek bone; but as it happened, I just swayed outside it and hit him with my own right cross on the point of the jaw. At that moment the sensation of a perfect connection — almost like an electric current — sped up my arm and I knew it was all over. The sailor probably came to that conclusion as well just before he spread himself on the floor and closed his eyes.

I stepped back and straightened my jacket and hat, then I lit a Camel. Gloria asked for one too; I told her they were strong but she said she'd smoked them before. After a while she said:

'There's a storeroom down the hall. The key's in the door.'

I shrugged. 'May as well.' I put the cigarette in my mouth then grabbed him under the shoulders and dragged him out into the little room. I locked the door.

Gloria handed me a glass of sherry. I told her the sailor seemed okay. She nodded and patted the bed for me to sit down beside her.

'So . . . what have you been doing with yourself since I last saw you,' she asked. 'Somebody told me you were closed down by the peelers. Then I heard you were inside; then I heard you were on the dole . . . I kept meaning to give you a call, but I suppose I was waiting for you to make the first move.'

'Well, I've made it now.'

'You certainly have.'

'But no, I haven't been closed down or inside and I'm definitely not on the dole — that's not my style.'

She smiled. 'You always did have class — I'll say that for you.'

'What's the story on this place?'

'Honestly, Bernie, I don't really know. Somehow Leslie — the sailor, as you call him — picked up the title to this pub. I'm sure he didn't buy it — well, not with his own money anyway — he's always been as broke as the rest of us. All I know is he invited me here and since he's either out gallivanting around the city or clean out of his mind with that junk he takes, it's been left to me to look after the place.'

'How profitable is that?'

'That's cheeky, Bernie,' she said, then pulled off my false beard and threw it across the room. 'And I thought you had some class. Keeping your beard on in a lady's bedroom . . . I never heard the like of it.'

I unlocked the door of the storeroom then stepped back as I jerked it open. The sailor was sitting against the wall. He said his head hurt.

'Come on out,' I said, feeling sorry for him. 'Let's go downstairs.'

The barman was just closing up. He emptied the ashtrays, wiped the bar top, then left without a look or a word. I poured two whiskies, gave one to the sailor. We sat down at a table.

'Why did you do this to me?' he asked softly.

I opened a new pack of Camels and reached one to him. 'Sometimes I don't know why I do things, sailor — not at the time anyway. Usually I can justify them later, in my own way. Sometimes, before doing something that's a little doubtful, I'll stop and think for a while — might be only ten seconds but I'll think about it. Upstairs you didn't even give me that long.'

'You had her on the bed and she —'

'Sailor,' I said firmly, 'she's not your property. She's a person in her own right and I didn't have to ask anyone's permission but hers.' I placed the glass in his hand. 'You'll feel better after a couple of these.'

After he'd drunk most of the bottle I asked him about the blonde. He pretended not to know anything about her so I backhanded him across the mouth. He stopped pretending and said he was working for some big shot called Buck McKaine, who had told him to deliver a small parcel to the blonde.

'What's this McKaine do?' I asked.

'Sells furniture.'

'And what else?'

'I don't know.'

'Like hell you don't. What else do you do besides leg-work?'

'Nothing. I just deliver things.'

'When's the last time you were in Dunglow?'

He was too drunk to contain his reaction. His head jerked up and for the first time his eyes showed fear. He said quietly: 'I don't know anything about it.'

'You're going to have a very sore face before I'm finished,' I said and hit him again.

He started to sob. 'The island. It was the island.'

'What's its name?' I shouted.

'Findargad. It's called Findargad. It's . . .' His voice trailed off and he started to rise from the chair. He threw a couple of pathetic little punches at me, then as he lurched towards the door I grabbed his arm to steady him. Realising that he was in no shape to reveal anything more, I led him upstairs and locked him in the storeroom.

The light was on but Gloria was sleeping, and I noticed that she'd finished off the sherry. I got out of my clothes, leaving them in a neat pile on a chair in case I needed to put my hands on them quickly, then I shook out the pillow and lay down beside her.

It had been a strange, tiring day — traipsing around after the sailor and virtually taking over the pub — but those are often the kind when one makes the most progress. Patience, undercover surveillance and tough tactics have been the staples of detective work since ancient times, and today they had resulted in my first major breakthrough. As I drifted off to sleep I felt pleased and confident, and was not a bit disconcerted by the recurring image of Dale Diamond and his sardonic smile.

Chapter 7
Shadow of the Professor

I was dreaming the sailor had brought me up a pint when I came awake with a jolt. It was a few seconds before I realised that Gloria had been prodding my side.

'Don't sleep all day, Bernie.' She lit a cigarette then said, yawning: 'My mouth . . . feels like the inside of one of those pipes you used to smoke. Ugghh!'

I looked at my watch: it was 9:30. 'Stay where you are,' I said, 'and I'll make some tea.'

I pulled on my socks, trousers and shirt, then padded out to the storeroom and opened the door. After a few moments the prisoner emerged; he looked like death warmed up and I felt like it. We trudged down the stairs into the darkened bar. I went on through to the kitchen and put on the kettle. When I returned to the bar, the sailor was pouring a vodka.

'I hope you're not at that till,' I said, half-jokingly. 'That's mine now.'

He gave me a pitiful look. 'The only thing I'm interested in is a drink.'

I opened the till. There was quite a lot of money in it; too much, I thought, to leave overnight in an area like this. I wondered at Gloria doing a thing like that.

'I'll take that, if you don't mind,' said Gloria, appearing suddenly behind me.

Feeling slightly offended, I turned round and gave her a sharp look. 'No need for that, you know,' I said. 'I was going to bring it up to you with the cup of tea.'

'I didn't want you to have the trouble,' she said, then smiled. 'Besides, I doubt if you could even have managed the tea on your own.'

I just smiled back and went out to unplug the kettle.

After breakfast Gloria admitted to a certain feeling of nausea and went back to bed. 'A good idea,' I told her, thinking that it was better if I had the sailor all to myself. She stayed there for the rest of the morning, reading, and watching the television he had carried in for her. It was an expensive model, but at one point, just as I was interrogating the sailor, she shouted down that it was going haywire. Annoyed at the interruption, I went up and examined the set. There appeared to be nothing wrong with it so I decided to check the aerial. Crossing to the window, I stuck my head out and looked up. The trouble had been located.

'It's those danged crows,' I told Gloria.

She looked at me for a few seconds then cast her eyes to the ceiling in apparent exasperation. 'Don't talk daft, Bernie,' she said and went back to her reading.

But what a strange sight it was: several crows were dancing up and down on the aerial and one was even swinging from it. The largest crow had spied me straight away and now he gave a caw and started to peck strongly at one of the rods. He looked down at me again with his head tilted to one side, gave another caw, then started to peck again. It was pure mischief on his part. Then his crow-cronies, probably following his example, began to caw and peck too, and soon they were all at it.

We'll soon see about this, I thought, and ran down the stairs. Within minutes I had the sailor out on the street firing up at them with a catapult previously confiscated from the local urchins. He was obviously enjoying his work and after several hopelessly wild shots and much raucous abuse from the sailor (I may not have been too far wrong in interpreting the chief crow's spirited cawing at this point as an equally scandalous response), they flapped away to another roof top just out of range.

Actually, I was surprised that the mere sight of the sailor had not been sufficient to shift them, because he'd been drunk for at least an hour. He came in singing:

'I'll tell my ma when I go home
The crows won't leave the teevee alone,'

and threw out a small baldy customer, accusing the man of looking at him. He started drilling up and down the landing with a broomstick and shooting at Germans from under Gloria's bed. He told one of the early whores he was a genuine Egyptian, making her scream out in anger when he tried to brush her away.

'Why did you lie to me?' he shouted at her. 'You told me this was a pyramid.'

He ran into the kitchen, sat on the hot range, jumped off that in a hurry, then opened the pantry door to go home.

'They've bricked up the back door,' he wailed, throwing himself onto a sack of flour. 'Oh my God, the humans are after me.'

There was quiet for a time as he made friends with a bag of potatoes, then he emerged looking subdued, putting down white floury footprints, and with tears running down his floury face. He sat down on the floor and looked at me balefully.

'I suppose you think I should be back in the asylum,' he said in a quiet voice.

'Perhaps, but I think the storeroom will suffice for the present.'

He looked puzzled at this, then his eyes lit up as if suddenly recalling the storeroom as an idyllic abode where he had once been very happy. As I led him up the stairs he chanted, 'The storeroom! The storeroom! I want to go back to the storeroom!'

Well, that's enough of this place, I thought, after returning the sailor to his room. I had wanted to extract more information from him but that was now obviously out of the question for several hours at least.

Surprisingly, with all the noise the sailor had been making, Gloria was asleep when I looked in to say goodbye.

'So long, Gloria,' I whispered, standing by the bed. 'I've got to go now. I don't want to, but there comes a time when a soldier-detective has to do what he has to do. I'll try and get back but, you see, there's something I have to do and it's possible I may not live to see this thing through . . . because it's a tough thing, a rough thing, a tall thing, a tricky thing —'

'Bernie,' she said, opening her eyes and smiling drowsily. 'I hope you're satisfied.' She turned over, apparently going back to sleep.

I kissed the back of her head. 'I'll give you a call,' I said. Then I picked up my hat and went out.

Needless to say, I felt rather pleased with myself as I walked briskly back to my car. I had discovered that a certain Buck McKaine was the employer of both the sailor and the blonde. And I had the name of a small island which the sailor, McKaine and, presumably,

Dunslaney had visited shortly after the date of the bank robbery. I imagined that there may well come a time when men will recall

The great day Bernard Holland took over the notorious Doxy's Tavern and discovered the clue that led him to the fabled Dunslaney fortune. He was the last private eye in Belfast but by far the best.

And as an old woman, after sobbing uncontrollably at the mention of his name, Gloria murmured, 'He was a brute, he was dangerous, but I worshipped him.'

As soon as I opened the door of the ground-floor office I knew that there were bad feelings in the air. Faye, sitting at my desk, regarded me coldly. (But even that could not suppress my pleasure at seeing her there.) Herman was standing against the back wall, looking small and agitated.

I hung up my hat. 'Sorry I'm late,' I said casually. 'Something came up . . . Now then, getting settled in all right, are we?' I gave her a nice smile; but she wasn't having that. She said, still glaring:

'Apparently your . . . your assistant here didn't know anything about me. He tried to manhandle me out of here. I had to knee the little get in the balls.'

'Herman!'

'And she kicked me in the stomach,' he growled.

'I'd say you deserved everything you got.' I strode over to him and jabbed him in the chest. 'Since when did you start pushing ladies around, eh? And in this office too —'

'He claims you didn't tell him I was starting today.'

'What? Of course I told him. I told him quite distinctly you would be here today. Probably forgot it or wasn't even listening in the first place.' I turned to Herman. 'Didn't you forget it?'

'Sorry, Bern,' he said morosely. His breath was stale with beer.

I had not, as I well knew, told him anything of the sort. I had intended to, but events overtook me, and it must have slipped my mind. But be that as it may, there was in my opinion still no excuse for his wretched behaviour.

I went over to Faye, who was examining her nylons for a run. For some reason I have always been stimulated by the sight of a woman with a run, particularly above the knee. I think perhaps that I associate it with wantonness. I said: 'He's been acting a little strangely these past few days —'

She looked up as someone entered. A customer, I thought, noticing a slight diffidence as he approached the desk: a welcome change from the steely manner I was so accustomed to in my visitors, who, for a recent period of about a year, had seemed to be either creditors or representatives of the authorities.

'I phoned yesterday,' he said. 'You asked me to call round today. It's about —'

'Let's go up to my other office,' I said, letting him know that he wasn't dealing with one of those one-room operations so common in every large city.

'That's a nice young lady,' he said shyly as we climbed the stairs.

'That's my executive assistant,' I said with a certain amount of pride. I was now considering Faye as my most valuable asset, a position formerly held by my stock of Pirelli calendars.

The rest of the afternoon saw me very busy meeting customers and answering the phone. During the relatively quiet spells I was able to give her an outline of my enterprises. She understood fully my rationalization of the more unorthodox aspects, nodding impatiently as if it all went without saying. I found it very refreshing to be once more in contact with an enlightened mind and she seemed almost pleased when I told her that. I did not, of course, refer to the case.

At six o'clock Faye and I were sitting around a bottle of Old Comber and I asked her what she thought. I was feeling fairly confident; apart from the earlier contretemps — Herman had been banished in disgrace — the afternoon had gone well.

'I think you're an interesting man,' she said. Her tone was a little detached, I thought: more like that of an observer than a participant. Still, it gave me pleasure. As far as I could recall, it was the nicest thing she had yet said to me.

The great airships lined out for ten leagues on either side of our flagship: a second horizon in the Vulcan sky.

On the prow stood I, Holland, with Spock at my right and John Carter at my left; my lady kneeling before me, her light green eyes scanning the line — now but twelve leagues distant and but half a league less in array — of the death hulks of the black-hooded quasi-gods, followers of the Professor.

'The fate of my planet and, indeed, the Federation is in your hands, Commander,' said Spock in a tone of hushed veneration.

'Aye, 'tis true,' said I, Holland; 'the future of the very Universe hinges on the success of my battle strategy. 'Tis a great responsibility.'

Admiration from Spock is admiration indeed, thought I, fleetingly. But now to battle.

'Enter attack plan *5232*, Mr. Carter.'

'Attack plan *5232* entered, Commander,' said Carter.

Aye, thought I, Holland, the Professor will pay tribute to me ere this Vulcan day is over.

★ ★ ★ ★ ★ ★

Images of the Professor come to me frequently in the night hours. His shadowy figure flits through the domain of my subconscious, taunting with an appearance that beckons me to close to him, then disappearing behind a web of his own spinning.

Able criminal, man of multiple identities and illusions — that is the Professor. I have sensed his hand in the perpetration of several notable crimes of the recent past. Morality, compassion and mercy are alien concepts to him; he has a heart of cold white flesh. Compared to his philosophy, that of Nietzsche ranks as one of loving philanthrophy.

I met him in Liverpool before the war; we were both in our late teens and he had just begun to perceive the possibilities of crime. Unknowingly, I allowed myself to be used by him as a courier of cocaine — I, in my innocence, thought it was Spanish Fly — and it was only with the greatest manoeuvring and luck that I managed to avoid prison.

I have encountered him several times since then, although in two instances I didn't realise it until afterwards — as in the case of the forged paintings. Indeed, I have reason to believe that he, and not Portuguese Joe, was the brains behind the hi-jacking of those two loads of cigarettes. It was not without significance, I thought afterwards, that Sergeant Murkley went on about a mysterious 'Billy' who was, he claimed, not only my employer but 'one of the craftiest mates in the country.' I think we were both assuming that 'Billy' was a man, but he could well have been referring to Billie, the Professor's wife and principal accomplice.

I had several customers that next morning, including two middle-aged hopefuls from the ranks of Belfast's love-lorn. I talked glibly enough about amatory aids and the perils of loneliness, but my mind wasn't on those things. I was thinking of Findargad. I had known over a day ago that it was necessary to go there, yet here I was, still in my office, stuck to my chair, not even believing my own reasons for delaying the trip. I decided to go that afternoon.

When I informed Faye that she would have to hold the fort for a day or two as I was going out of town on business, she replied that she had a long-standing dentist's appointment after lunch and would not be back until after three o'clock. She wondered if I could possibly contemplate delaying my departure until such time as she could return with all due haste. I decided that she was adopting rather a sardonic tone for one proposing to absent herself for several hours on only her second day at work; however, I had no real option but to agree, and with a forced good grace at that.

After a light lunch I settled back in my swivel chair, a glass of Old Comber before me, and let my thoughts wander idly over the possible consequences of embarking on this Findargad adventure.

The next move seemed fairly straightforward: I had to drive out to Dunglow, make my way to the island, then attempt to find the location described in the document. The only snag, I thought, was that such an apparent lack of complication was not compatible with my experience of life, and I wondered at which point on that simple itinerary would I receive the usual kick in the teeth. But I soon dismissed my misgivings. I had been in this position many times before and I knew that the greatest obstacle to success is often one's own fear and doubts. A kick in the teeth is a very small injury compared to the debilitating effect of a weak spirit.

I poured the last drink from the bottle, blew into it to make a foghorn noise, then drank a toast to a remarkably interesting case. I thought of Marcus Dunslaney, staring out from the cold waters of the Atlantic; Faye, his daughter, aloof yet alluring; Portuguese Joe, sweaty, shifty and dangerous; Gloria, dark, accessible, and a woman with a past; the sailor, tormented and none-too-bright; Dolan, the villain who looks like me; the slinky blonde, who uses her body as a trap; Sergeant Murkley, the cop who hates me; Buck McKaine, the respectable businessman with so much to hide; and the Professor, perhaps the most evil man in the world.

I thought of lonely barren islands lashed by the howling waters of the ocean; of sirens, blonde and beautiful, enticing with enchanting and dreadful sounds; of treasures, and hulking pirates with the faces of Dolan and Murkley and Portuguese Joe, who laugh and taunt as I dig my own grave.

Chapter 8
The quick-change artist

The Atlantic region of Donegal is rugged and sparsely populated; and although Dunglow is only a smallish market town and port, it is the business and entertainment centre for a fairly large area. I had visited the town once before, several years earlier, and to my knowledge the best place to stay was the Armada Hotel, attractively situated on a promontory at the outskirts of the town.

It was dark when I drove up the tree-lined lane to the hotel. It had, I remembered, thirty or thirty-five rooms and about twenty acres of grounds, mostly wooded and bounded at the north by the ocean. I parked under a lamp-post in the spacious but crowded carpark, using the light to apply a beard — the one equivalent to about three weeks' growth. Then I went in and registered under the name of Homer Wilkinson.

After depositing my suitcase in the room I made a tour of the hotel, recalling the general lay-out and, in particular, memorising the exits. Then I went out to my car and drove back along the lane onto the main road. There was a side road a couple of hundred yards further down and I went along that until I found a shoulder. I parked there, locked the car, and walked back to the hotel.

In the banquet room, on the ground floor, there was a party in progress. It seemed to be a private affair: a celebration or reunion. The room was very crowded but with unerring instinct I pushed my way through to the bar. I fixed a gin and lemonade, then stood for a time watching the guests, most of whom were in groups of two's or three's, cigarette in one hand, drink in the other, and talking into each other's faces.

I was smiling at this when I felt a hard jolt in the small of my back. I froze for a moment or two, then realising that it wasn't a gun or knife, I turned slowly round. A young man with light curly hair looked at me anxiously; he mumbled 'sorry' and turned towards the drinks table. Then, for about thirty seconds, he just stared down at the bottles and glasses as if he didn't know what to do with them.

I heard a girl shout, 'Gordon! Hurry up with those drinks!' He, apparently, was Gordon, for the girl's voice brought him instantly to life — or, more precisely, put him in a panic. He knocked over glasses, got down to pick them up, banged his head on the table as he rose, knocking down more glasses, banged his head again.

'Gordon! What the hell are you doing? You're a one-man disaster area.'

The voice, I was almost certain, belonged to one of two young women who were sitting on the carpet, against the wall. Both were dark and each of them was as attractive as the other, though in a different way.

I returned my attention to Gordon, who by this time had managed to fill two glasses with what appeared to be gin and tonic. However, while this may have represented on his part a feat of co-ordination preceded by either a sudden recall of the girls' order or a bold decision to improvise, there was no certainty or even, as I realised watching him back into a plump woman, any likelihood of the drinks surviving the ten paces required to deliver them into the hands of the impatient girls. And, as it happened, turning round, presumably with the intention of apologising to the plump woman, he succeeded only in upsetting one of the drinks over her shoulder.

Realising that it would be a few minutes before he could disembarrass himself from that situation, I decided to accept responsibility for the task at which he had failed so miserably, and in a fluent practised manner I fixed two gin and tonics and carried them over to the girls.

'What about Levi-Strauss, then?' I asked, utilising one of the more esoteric of my gambits. They both laughed and I added: 'I was watching your friend; he seemed to need a little help in the highly complex operation of mixing tonic with gin.'

We all laughed at that; then the one with the long hair said: 'Where did you spring from?'

'Liverpool University,' I replied; that being my cover.

'Did you hear that, Charlene? A professor from Liverpool.'

Charlene regarded me with her blue Irish eyes. 'What's your subject?' she said.

'Actually, I'm involved in some rather important research at the moment regarding the development of a new literary genre.'

'That's lovely . . . hey, there's another professor of literature over there. You might have a chat with him later.'

'No, I won't bother,' I said. 'Don't like to talk shop at parties.'

I offered cigarettes and as we lit up, Gordon approached clutching two drinks. 'Basically, what happened was . . . this woman . . . well, first of all, I couldn't recall —'

'Oh, shut up, Gordon,' snapped Charlene. 'We'd absolutely *die* of thirst waiting for you.'

Gordon, who appeared to exist in a continual state of blushing, bent over with the drinks. The other girl caught him by the ear. 'Sit here, Gordon, and amuse us for a while.' She pulled him down until he rested on his knees, then said to me:

'This chap works with us, Professor — *if* you can call it work, that is. What he *really* does is drive everybody to distraction with his bungling and complete lack of commonsense. I ask you, what does it say for your fellow professors that they'd award the like of that a B.A.?' This was said not maliciously but with a glint of amusement in her eyes; it seemed that tormenting the unspeakable Gordon was almost a pastime of theirs.

I had to agree, adding that Laurel and Hardy were efficient sensible men compared to Gordon. With this encouragement they became more daring in their maltreatment of him: they speculated on various surgical treatments for his condition, and in particular what had gone amiss in the brain operation he had supposedly undergone. They contemplated hanging him on the door to their room to compensate for the metal numeral he had apparently knocked down that afternoon — his function being to shout 'Good evening, this is room one-eleven' whenever someone approached. (Was this, I wondered, a device to inform me of their room number?)

And, though some may not regard this as maltreatment at all, they each forced him to drink a glass of gin and tonic from one of their shoes.

All this was of course fairly interesting as far as it went, but after a time I found myself becoming increasingly irritated; the source of my impatience was not, I must admit, the whimsical abuse they were directing at him but rather the fact that, pathetic though he was, Gordon had been from the moment he arrived the centre of attraction.

My glass was now empty so I made my way back to the bar and poured a giant gin. After a couple of gulps of that I felt obliged to caution myself about overindulging on a case. I have enough trouble trying to control my drinking when I have to pay for it, let alone when it's free.

'What's the party for?' I asked a creature hunched over the bar. He had long blond hair tied in a tail, a small ring in one ear, and a moustache that completely covered his mouth.

'Some dude's got himself hitched,' he said, and tittered. 'That's one trip I ain't too anxious to go on, believe me, man.' He picked up a drink and moved away chuckling. If he had stayed I might have told him about my own wedding party, which was a grand event all right, but I still regret the fact that it was the highlight of my marriage.

Three days and three nights was the length of my party. We drank one hundred gallons of beer, sixty bottles of wine and fifty bottles of spirits. There were three ceilidh bands and two poets. Twelve people were arrested (including me), seven went to hospital, four became engaged and there were three subsequent separations. There were seven knock-down fights where we made a ring, and I don't know how many brawls in the street. Eight people lost jobs because of it and four people got jobs because of it. Three cars, two motorbikes and one house (my mother-in-law's) were wrecked. Fourteen songs (nine in my honour) were composed, thirteen poems, twelve reels, and a prayer.

And when those who were there are old and gnarled and warming at the fire, a tiny grandchild might climb upon a knee and say: 'What did you do in life, Grandda?' Then the old man will proudly reply: 'Child, I was at Bernard Holland's wedding party.'

(Two points are perhaps worth mentioning: firstly, one of the poems to which I referred was composed by me over a period of several months prior to the wedding. It was a long poem — over one hundred pages — intended as a chronicle of my experiences as a contractor on the building sites of England immediately after the war, and in particular my struggle with the Corkmen and Culshie Mucks which culminated in the pitched battle of Birkenhead in 1948. However, when I tried to recite it to the assembled company there was not one person artistic enough or, for that matter, courteous enough to listen past page ten.

Secondly, while getting arrested on one's wedding day may well be regarded as indicating a lack of consideration for one's wife, I would submit that it is far more indicative of a serious lack of empathy on the part of the police.)

Suddenly tiring of its cloying atmosphere, I pushed my way out of the banquet room and sauntered down to the hotel bar.

'A gin and lemonade, if you please,' I said jauntily to the barman, and climbed onto a stool. In keeping with the name of the hotel the room had a nautical theme: wooden beams, nets, hanging lanterns, ships' wheels, captains' hats, ropes, old-time compasses, stuffed seagulls, sextants, shells. A little over-done perhaps but it was pleasant to sit there and imagine one could hear and smell the nearby ocean.

I spent a quiet twenty minutes just nursing my drink and thinking about things in general. Then the barman, with whom I had had a brief conversation, started to chuckle. I looked up and caught his eye. Still smiling, he leaned over, nodded in a direction behind me and said in a low voice:

'That Mr. Holland, he's a real character if there ever was one. You know, this afternoon . . .'

I didn't hear the rest. I didn't hear anything as I looked over my shoulder at a sight which seemed to strike me like a blow.

Strolling majestically across the bar, a pretty girl on each arm, was a man I had last seen under very different circumstances. It was Dolan.

Chapter 9

Excursions of a Sailor-Detective

'Are you all right, sir?' asked the barman, referring to the shock that must have shown on my face.

I nodded. 'Yes, perfectly all right . . . What about Mr. Holland?'

'Excuse me a second,' he said and went to serve another customer. A minute later he returned. 'Where were we, now?' he said softly. 'Ah, yes — Mr. Holland. Came into the bar this morning, shortly after we opened. Weren't too many people here at that time and we got into talking. Oh, you should have heard the lines that man came out with. What a talker! Had us in stitches, so he did.' He started to whisper. 'After a few drinks he showed us his card, and you'd never guess what he does.

He's a private detective — from Belfast, no less; and what's more, he said that with the Troubles and all he's now the last private detective in that city.'

While he was telling me this I had kept my eye on Dolan. He had crossed with his entourage to the entrance and was standing there talking to the women. A strikingly beautiful redhead came up to him, he whispered something in her ear, she giggled. Then the four of them went out.

I followed them. I was just in time to see Dolan enter the banquet room, but when I reached the door they had been swallowed up by the crowd. They'll head for the bar, I thought, and started to push my way through. A hand gripped my shoulder; the shock of it jerked me round, ready to strike out.

It was Charlene. She backed off, her eyes wide with alarm, staring at my grim face. I turned away, and as I did so I caught a flash of red hair. I moved towards it as fast as I could. She was standing with the two other women, but I still couldn't see Dolan.

Then he emerged from behind the redhead. He was shaking with laughter and some of his drink spilled onto the floor. I heard the redhead say, 'Oh, Bernie . . .' and then her lips just moved as the noise of the crowd drowned out the rest. I stared at him for maybe a minute, seeing him as he stood in my office with a revolver in his hand, saying 'Goodbye, sucker.' For the hundredth time in the past five minutes I tried to work out why the police had released him, why he was free to come after me again. If he had escaped he wouldn't be here now, flaunting himself under the name of a man he tried to murder. I didn't know what all this meant but I knew what I had to do. The din of the crowd seemed to fade away, and as I watched Dolan laughing and fondling the redhead's arm, I knew I had to kill him.

Suddenly, the room was plunged into darkness. For

a moment there was silence, then the sound of a shot roared: deafening, painful; the strong smell of cordite; another second of silence, now eerie, shocked; then screaming, the sound of people panicking, rushing to get out. Somebody knocked heavily against me; then the jolts and pressure of more bodies against mine. I struggled to keep my balance.

The lights snapped on. Within seconds I was clear of the mass of bodies surging towards the doors. I gripped the bar table and looked down at Dolan. He had been shot in the face at point-blank range.

I backed away, my brain numb except for the strange feeling that I was looking at my own corpse. Then, as if galvanised by this sensation, I jerked around and joined the throng, pushing, shoving, jostling. As I neared a door I was knocked against a wall, and as that happened I felt the pain of something small and hard crushing against my side. Instinctively I reached into my jacket pocket and my fingers closed around the warm muzzle of a revolver.

Now my desire to escape intensified. Like a madman I forced my way into the corridor. The crowd was moving towards the lobby so I ran in the opposite direction, towards a rear exit. Rounding a corner I tripped over something, went sprawling and banged my head against a wall. Although in considerable pain I got up immediately and looked at the object that had nearly ruined my escape. It was Gordon. He was down on all-fours with one hand outstretched feeling for his spectacles, which lay several feet in front of him. I felt like stomping on them but I contented myself with sinking my boot into his backside. Then I was running again, down the corridor and through the exit that led onto the back enclosure.

Suddenly, a man appeared, several yards in front of me. He was holding a gun and it was pointed at me, so

I stopped.

'Walk in front of me. I'll tell you where to go.' The voice was 'upper-class' English.

I began to walk. The blow I had taken on the head was affecting me; I couldn't think. My mind reverberated with the booming rhythm of the words 'Walk in front of me. I'll tell you where to go'; over and over again.

'Through those trees.'

Then, after we'd passed through them and reached a patch of open ground, my head began to clear. I could tell by the sound of his footsteps that he was keeping just two or three paces behind; on account of that, I felt it would be foolish to attempt to pull my new-found gun or make a break for it: he could have shot me down in an instant. We went through another clump of small trees and now I could see the edge of a cliff dropping to the ocean.

'Stop here. Turn around.'

I paused for a few moments, conscious for the first time of the fresh salty wind and the beat of the waves. I looked at the stones and the sparse grass on the cliff top; I looked at the ocean, and the sky; and then, with a feeling of immeasurable sadness, I turned to face my probable executioner.

His face was clearly visible in the moonlight. He was young and darkly handsome, his brown eyes expressionless.

'That was a nasty business back there, Mr. Wilkinson,' he said. He gave a grim smile. 'Or should I say, Mr. Holland?'

I said nothing, just kept looking at him and, in the periphery of my vision, his revolver.

'I want the document, Mr. Holland.'

I shook my head.

He sighed, then said urgently: 'We haven't much time. This area will soon be thick with police. My name is Peppar — Major Peppar. I am acting on behalf of British Intelligence. I need that document and as this is a matter of national importance, you are obliged to give it to me. Make no mistake, I have the authority to dispose of anyone who stands in my way. Are you going to force me to do that?'

I shook my head again. 'I'll give it to you.' Slowly, I pulled an envelope from the breast pocket of my jacket and tossed it to him.

Still covering me, he opened the envelope and started to read, glancing up at me every few seconds. Apparently satisfied, he placed the document in his pocket and said: 'Where's the original?'

'In my office.'

He stared at me for several seconds. 'I hope you're playing straight with me, Mr. Holland, because we shall be meeting again.'

I nodded. 'Yes, I realise that. I know what the consequences would be.' Then I added: 'There'll be an awful diplomatic row if you're caught in the Republic.'

He ignored that. 'What are you planning to do now?' he said.

'Go back to Belfast.'

He stood very still for a few moments as if listening for the sound of someone approaching, then: 'I suggest that you leave now.'

I looked pointedly at the revolver. 'Go on,' he urged. 'I'm not going to shoot you in the back.'

I still felt very exposed as I walked slowly away. When I reached the trees I looked back, and he was gone. I sat down on a log and using my jacket to hide the light I lit a cigarette, inhaling the smoke greedily. I started to feel a little dizzy, then the next thing I knew I was chuckling noiselessly. God damn it, Peppar, did you really think it was that easy?

★ ★ ★ ★ ★ ★

The fact that the police would now be looking for a bearded Professor Wilkinson did not overly concern me. I was confident that I could elude them for the time required to cross over to Findargad and get back across the border. I regarded the police as the least of my worries; even with the elimination of Dolan there were far more dangerous enemies to contend with. But now I was armed, and the fact that the revolver was blooded made it seem even more potent. There were only four rounds in the Chief's Special, but if there was any shooting to be done I was determined to make each one count.

About a mile from the hotel I arrived at the main road. That stretch was deserted so I ran across, climbed over a low stone wall and set off over the fields on a course that would eventually lead to my car.

An hour later, as I gazed over the moon-lit countryside, trying to work out my position, I wondered whether my course had been just a little too circuitous. That's not to say I was lost. In fact, it was a deliberate manoeuvre based on the theory that if you don't know yourself where you're going then it's almost impossible for your pursuers to work out your intentions and intercept you.

(One of my wartime mottoes summed up the whole idea beautifully; a motto that in 1942 I offered to Stirling for the newly-formed SAS. Apparently, Confuse the Enemy with the Unexpected was considered a little lengthy, and he opted instead for Who Dares, Wins. Later, realising that adopting Confuse the Enemy with the Unexpected would be tantamount to broadcasting to the Germans the guiding principle of SAS operations, I came to agree with that decision. Particularly so when I considered the opposition Stirling's plans faced from Allied commanders, some of whom tended to be infuriatingly orthodox.

My own superiors were certainly orthodox; they used to get very shirty when, applying my principle to them, I deliberately mislead them about what I was doing. That episode at Ardglass — which may well be regarded as a key chapter of *Case-Histories of a Soldier-Detective* — seemed to be just the chance they were waiting for. Although I was not summarily dismissed, when I did leave the service shortly afterwards it was, so to speak, under a small but remarkably dogged cloud. Now, of course, I am completely vindicated: now that it has been revealed that a goodly portion of British Intelligence was working for the Soviets.)

Two hours later, as I trudged up the grassy slope of a hill, my legs gave way. I rolled over onto my back and lay there sucking in the fresh night air. After a minute or two my breathing returned to normal. I sat up and lit a scruffy-looking Camel from my battered pack. The dark quiet ocean stretched out below; to the east the lights of Dunglow — few that they were — danced and did tricks in the haze of my tiredness. Sitting there, high in the warm countryside, the events of the day seemed remote, almost part of a different world. It seemed strange that I could just walk away from everything and find this peace.

It was still dark when I jerked awake. I listened for a short time to a few birds chirping and singing in the trees below, then I stood up and performed several stretching exercises; my joints creaked and cracked but it helped to relieve some of the stiffness in my back and legs.

So the old trooper dozed off for a while, eh? I wasn't too pleased about that. Apart from the danger of being surprised, falling asleep on the ground was something a man of my age should have been careful to avoid — no matter how tired he was.

The sky over the horizon was starting to lighten as

I finally approached my car. I felt dirty, my mouth was dry and foul-tasting, and I would have given half of Dunslaney's hoard for a hot bath and a mug of sweet scalding tea.

I was walking along the side road on which I had parked my Zodiac when a sudden realisation stopped me in my tracks. Last night in the hotel a man calling himself Bernard Holland was killed. The police would contact the address in the hotel register — a pound to a penny it was mine — and Mrs. Holland would be notified of her husband's tragic murder. Even when they sent the body to her she wouldn't suspect anything. Dolan had looked remarkably like me, in build, in features — and the disfigurement of his face would make it unlikely that she would realise the corpse was not mine.

I decided to give this matter some serious thought. An opportunity to get rid of that harridan after all these years was not to be discarded lightly; and until I made my decision I thought it wise to keep away from everyone who knew me. I had on occasion considered faking my own demise — leaving a pile of clothes on some beach, then taking off for Canada, where in 1953 I acquired landed immigrant status — but I never got round to actually doing it. This situation, however, seemed perfect. I couldn't have engineered it better if I'd tried.

The prospect of giving my wife the slip put new life into my steps and in less than five minutes I reached the car. The first thing I did was change into the brown cotton suit I'd placed on the back seat before leaving. Then I cleaned my face and shoes, combed my hair, and donned a brown moustache — I had discarded the beard soon after leaving Peppar. My next priority was finding something to eat.

The Comfy Cafe didn't look like much on the outside — the green paint was peeling off the woodwork, and the window had so many smears it was almost opaque. But I didn't care about the decor, and it wouldn't have mattered if I had: once I caught the smell of bacon and sausages as I approached the place my body just walked in of its own accord. Nothing short of a knife in the back would have stopped it.

I gave the elderly waitress the biggest order she'd had in a month of Sundays — steak, three eggs, a double portion of bacon and a pot of tea. While that was being prepared I went into the lavatory, filled the handbasin with hot water and soaked my aching feet for about two minutes each.

My breakfast was waiting when I returned, and as I dug into it I looked up once or twice to see the waitress staring at me with large respectful eyes.

After the table was cleared I took out my map and checked once more the location of Findargad. The island, about two miles long and a mile wide, lay five miles out from Dunglow. It appeared to be uninhabited: there were no roads or settlements marked on the map. But even if there were people on it — fishermen or men on the same quest as myself — I considered it large enough to provide cover for me as I searched for the reference points noted in the document.

Next on the agenda was the acquisition of a boat. I paid the waitress then set off down the sloping main street towards the waterfront. Though only nine o'clock the morning was bright and warm, the sky was cloudless and there was almost no breeze.

There were only three vessels moored alongside the stone quay. But after I gave an old man ten pounds he said it would be all right if I used one of them, an ancient motorboat that seemed barely seaworthy.

There was a look of wonderment in his eyes as I cast off and waved goodbye. I think it was the first time he'd seen anybody go out in an open boat wearing a suit, a dress hat, and carrying a spade. I put-putted along the coast for about a mile, getting used to the controls, then I headed out to sea.

The sun was warmer now and the wind was mild but invigorating. I felt carefree and flush, revelling in the feel of the ocean and shouting 'Standby to repel boarders, Mr. Hornblower!' each time a seagull approached or just whenever I felt like shouting it.

Then, as I peered ahead, the horizon changed shape. I gave a whoop and waved my hat in the air. I had sighted land.

Findargad, as it loomed up, was shaped like a jaggy-backed whale, rising at its highest to about five hundred feet. As I closed in I could make out several rocky coves. I headed towards them and then saw a stretch of stony beach sheltered by a cliff.

I tied up in a small inlet several yards from the end of the beach. With the spade over my shoulder I walked along the shingle and up a sharp slope, stopping to gaze over the heather-covered landscape of Findargad. Then I climbed to the top of the nearest ridge, about two hundred yards from where I had landed, and consulted the document. I was looking for three trees in a row pointing towards the gap between two hills. There was nothing like that in sight, so I started to tramp towards an area of high ground half a mile away.

Eventually I reached the nearest of the hills. I climbed to the top, but again could not see the row of trees. I sat down to take a rest. My shirt was soaked with sweat and my trousers were sticking to my legs. I had been puffing quite hard coming up the hill and I didn't relish the thought of trudging much more, up and down, through that tiring heather. Wearily I got to my feet to resume the search.

And then I saw them. Three short trees in a gully at the bottom. It must have been a trick of the light, I thought, that prevented me from seeing them minutes earlier. But no matter; they were visible now and I was so excited I ran down the slope.

According to the document I had to dig to a depth of one foot at a point midway between the two trees nearest to the hills. My excitement was almost feverish as I struck the ground with my spade and dug and dug and dug . . .

There was nothing there. I should have known it when I started to dig because that ground had not been disturbed in a long time. I pulled out the document, checked the instructions again. There was no mistake: this was the place. I dug wider, then dug in the other gap between the trees. I dug for well over an hour. But there was nothing there.

I was now exhausted, dirty and very hot. I rested for a long time, trying not to feel too downhearted; but I was unable to suppress a feeling of intense despondency. I grabbed the spade and threw it as far as I could into the heather, then I picked up my hat and walked slowly away.

But my troubles were not yet over; for as I discovered when I reached the beach, the boat was no longer there.

Chapter 10

Play it again, Gilfurphy

Intentionally or not, the cabin had been well concealed. On three sides there were trees and the front was against the side of a steep hill. Unless you happened to stumble upon it, it would have been almost impossible to spot — even from the air. It was night but no light showed through the window. Rain ran in torrents down the roof, collecting on the stony ground beneath to such an extent that the cabin was in danger of being flooded.

The night was cold for that time of year. The wind was high, driving the rain and swaying the lightly-rooted trees; the sea could be heard, loud in its surging and thrusting against the walls of the nearby cliffs; an unknown animal was wailing in the trees — or perhaps it was just the wind; the night was getting darker as the heavy storm clouds filled the sky; and, crouched on the hillside, a desperate man was staring grimly at the cabin.

That was me. I was desperate because I hadn't eaten in thirteen hours and I was cold and very wet. After discovering that my boat was gone I had tramped around the island, meeting no-one, and eventually becoming so weary that it was nothing but will-power that kept me going. Then I chanced upon the cabin.

It looked deserted, but I wasn't taking any chances. Hunched low and keeping away from the window, I eased soundlessly down the slope. Standing in front of the frail-looking door, I pulled out my revolver, listened for a few seconds for any sounds inside the cabin, then kicked as hard as I could against the lock. Immediately I threw myself to one side, flattening my chest against the outside wall. The door banged heavily against some object inside, flew back and forward several times, then creaked to a stop. I stood very still.

'Come in, Holland, before you get wet.'

My fingers tightened around the revolver. The voice rang out again: 'Do come in and close the door, there's a good man.'

I stepped into the doorway and looked in. A dark figure seemed to form at the back of the cabin. I pointed my revolver at it and took two steps forward.

'Put the pistol down, Holland,' said the voice, now behind me. 'I have a much more powerful one pointed straight at your back.'

I was in trouble, but I wasn't sure how much. I placed the Chief's Special on the floor and then with my hands well away from my side, turned slowly round. Standing against the wall, wearing a short leather jacket and with a fat revolver in his hand, was the man who called himself Major Peppar.

'You really are a tiresome fellow, Holland.'

'Look here, Peppar —'

'Shut up!' His eyes glared into mine. 'I haven't

decided yet what I'm going to do with you, but I'm beginning to agree with our friend over there that I should have pulled you in at the start and beat the truth out of you.'

I had already come to a conclusion about the silent figure behind me. Instinct, perhaps, but there was no doubt in my mind as I turned round to look upon his face.

Lounging on a pile of sacks, wearing a trenchcoat and a beret, an unlit cigarette dangling from his mouth, was that squalid freebooter, Portuguese Joe.

As I stared at him I could feel my mouth drawing back in a savage half grin. 'Ten seconds alone with you, chum, that's all I want —'

'Raise your hands above your head,' snapped Peppar. 'And don't be so hostile to our portly friend; he's in enough trouble already.'

I raised my hands. 'So you fouled up, eh, Joe?'

He didn't answer; he just sat there watching as Peppar searched me. The Englishman was quick but thorough. He felt in my hat, my armpits, in the small of my back, between my legs and even had me take my shoes off. He sniffed the end of my revolver then placed it in the pocket of his jacket.

'That's probably the gun that killed Dolan,' sneered Portuguese Joe.

'Without any doubt,' said Peppar; then he switched on a small flashlight and started to look at the document he had just taken from me.

Portuguese Joe gave an ugly laugh and drawing his hand across his throat, said: 'You know what happens to people who double-cross British Intelligence, don't you?'

I said: 'Doesn't sound like you're in so great with the major, yourself.'

'All right,' said Peppar, 'sit down and tell me the full story. But I warn you, make very sure that you tell me no lies, and leave nothing whatsoever out.'

So, with the aid of quite a few promptings, I gave him a fairly detailed non-incriminating version of the truth. I denied that I had ever intended to keep anything I found; all I wanted to do, I said, was make my name as a detective.

As could be predicted, Joe was highly sceptical. 'Look, Major, he could have known we had him under surveillance from the time he landed. That digging about near the trees could have been a ruse. Then when it got dark he went to the real location —'

'You were watching me? So you took the boat?'

He nodded with satisfaction. 'Come on, Major, we could have the truth out of him in five minutes.'

But Peppar wasn't listening. He motioned for us to be quiet. 'I think there's somebody out there,' he whispered, moving towards the door. As he passed me I slipped the Chief's Special from his pocket.

We remained very still and waited. I was conscious once more of the sound of the storm, but I could detect no other movement. We waited for what seemed to be several minutes until, slowly, the door began to open.

The shape of a man was just discernible as he paused in the doorway. Suddenly, the light from his torch glared and my hand tightened around the revolver. Then Peppar was upon him, the cabin went dark, a shot blasted out, a cry; then just the sound of the storm, the ringing after-effects of the shot and Peppar's heavy breathing.

He dragged the body into the cabin, then reached for the flashlight that had fallen to the floor. I looked down as he shone the beam into the man's face. He was beefy, with cropped hair and white scars around his eyebrows. I couldn't recall having seen him before.

Peppar said: 'He's not dead. That was his pistol that went off. Help me tie him up.'

There was a bundle of cord near the sacks; with a

pocket knife I cut off lengths and handed them to the major; again he did a quick and thorough job. Peppar seemed to be good at the incidentals of Intelligence work like searching, unarmed combat and tying up captives, but I was still reserving judgement about his proficiency in the larger, more vital aspects.

'Let's get out of here,' said Peppar.

I put up the collar of my jacket — for all the good that was going to do — and followed them out into the night. Fortunately the storm had subsided a little; the rain still pelted down but the wind had dropped considerably.

We plodded along the valley, sometimes up to our knees in mud and water, until we reached higher ground. Then Peppar picked up the pace. I kept going as best I could in the foul conditions, stopping only when I fell down, but I just couldn't keep up with the major. After five minutes I was gasping for every breath, my legs were like lead and I was covered in mud. My only consolation was that Portuguese Joe appeared to be in even worse shape. Lagging behind me, he was puffing and blowing, and begging Peppar to slow down. Twice we had to pull him out of bog holes.

Later, when Peppar was momentarily out of sight, Joe slipped on a steep slope and rolled about ten yards into a stream. There he lay on his face, entirely motionless. He must have been within an ace of drowning when I got to him and pulled him out by the feet. I helped him sit up and then, just to make sure he wasn't choking, slapped him as hard as I could on the back.

'Peppar doesn't give a fuck about his men,' he gasped. Then he looked at me with surprised, grateful eyes.

I patted the top of his head. 'I didn't want it that way, Portuguese. I'm saving you for later.'

Eventually we reached the boat — my boat — which was bobbing about ominously in a small inlet. The storm seemed suddenly to have become more violent.

'We can't go out in these conditions,' shouted Joe. 'We'd never make it.'

'Stay here then, you fat fool,' shouted Peppar over his shoulder; then he climbed into the motorboat and started to cast off.

Both Joe and I ran down the slope to the boat. As I stumbled in and Joe almost fell in, Peppar watched us with a stony glare.

'You'd be in better shape if you didn't smoke so much,' he grunted.

We headed out to sea, making very slow progress at first as the waves swept over us, and Portuguese Joe and I bailing furiously with our hats. Then the sea became much calmer and we no longer seemed in imminent danger of sinking. It felt good to be still alive. I felt that my luck had not entirely deserted me.

'How come,' I asked Peppar, 'we're taking my boat back. I mean, how did you two get to the island?'

'By submarine, Holland; how else?'

'Up you too,' I muttered.

A thin dawn was visible when, two hours later, we approached the mainland. I was shivering violently and now feeling nauseated instead of hungry. But suddenly, as I gazed at the other two, I found myself laughing. Peppar looked warily at me and I managed to say, 'Don't worry, I'm not cracking up. I was just thinking what a remarkably muddy and miserable-looking crew we were.' But it appeared that I was the only one who found that thought amusing.

As we went ashore at Dunglow we received all sorts of looks from the fishermen on the quay. Most people who live in small towns will stare at anything, but we undoubtedly made a strange picture as we trudged in Indian file along the harbour.

Both Peppar and Portuguese Joe were in filthy moods. Near the town centre Joe collapsed on a bench and vowed he was finished with British Intelligence; he said that Peppar was an aristocratic oaf, a bungler, and almost certainly a pederast. With a scowl, Peppar grabbed him by the collar and shook him mightily. Portuguese Joe's head vibrated at a great rate, especially his chins, and he spluttered for mercy: '. . . Just over . . . overwrought, ma, ma, major . . .' Peppar let go of him and walked away.

It was at this point, while Peppar was striding ahead and Joe was recovering his composure, that I decided to part company with my two companions.

I was still in some doubt as to the relation between Peppar and myself: although I now regarded him as a representative of the authorities, I definitely did not consider myself to be his prisoner. Peppar had absolutely no authority over me while we were in the Irish Republic; indeed, he was in no small danger of being arrested himself. Nevertheless, I felt it would be prudent to take my leave unannounced. The dictates of international law would be feeble protection against a blast from that small cannon of his — which I now knew to be a .44 Magnum.

So I just walked away, turned a corner, ran up a side street, through an alley, paused to get my bearings, then set off quickly in the general direction of my car.

It was, I suppose, naive of me to imagine that the Zodiac would still be where I'd parked it. After spending half an hour in a fruitless search of the area around the hotel I sat down on a grass verge and pondered what to do next.

The main thing, of course, was to get out of Dunglow

before I was arrested. It was also necessary to acquire new clothes: I couldn't get on a bus or hitch a lift looking like a man who had spent half the night tramping through wet and mud and the other half out in an open boat. But where do you get clothes at 7 a.m. on a Sunday? I thought about that for a while, then decided reluctantly that I would have to break into a men's outfitter.

It seemed like I was kicking in a lot of doors on this case. The back door of Crosbie's little shop swung open at the fourth strike. Twenty minutes later I was washed and looking good in black slacks, white shirt, black tie with brown stripes, grey sports jacket, a fawn raincoat and a grey dress hat; the shoes were my own. Transferring my personal effects, I checked my wallet; there was £68 left. I calculated the wholesale value of the clothes and placed £30 beside the cash register.

Then I headed out of town looking for somewhere to sleep. I was so tired I didn't even feel hungry anymore. I was so tired I would have laid down with a red-lipped vampire in a bed the Professor had rigged to tip me into a pit of wild-eyed bank robbers, hanging judges and Intelligence men with .44 Magnums and twitchy fingers. I considered that scenario for a while and somehow it didn't seem all that fanciful.

I was now in that state of superexhaustion in which the senses seem especially acute: the sound of cars passing was a roar and the groups of people strolling back from Chapel wore clothes that were too bright and had faces that were red and lined and revealing.

The corrugated-iron outhouse at the end of the farm lane seemed almost beautiful with the sun sitting on its roof as if guiding me to it. I made one last effort, calling the time to my steps. It was open. There were metal containers inside and rags that had once been blankets. I threw my raincoat down and slowly collapsed upon it.

The petrol fumes and the musty smell of animals did not disturb me as I drifted off to sleep.

It was after six o'clock when I woke up. The first thing I was conscious of was the stench that seemed to be crawling up my nostrils. I got up quickly, shook out the raincoat, and then started back to town.

I had decided to return to Belfast to lie low and recuperate, but from what the man at the bus company said, the only 'long-distance' bus that evening was one to Ballybofery, a small town twenty miles inland. That was the right direction at least, and as it was leaving in fifteen minutes I decided to take it.

I think the double-decker to Ballybofery had been purchased by the bus company after it had been retired from service in some part of India. I started off on the top deck but I began to feel seasick up there so I went downstairs and sat at the back near the emergency exit.

For most of the journey the bus crawled along at an unsteady 25 mph, stopping now and again to pick up and discharge passengers. Curiously, the only time the driver went above that speed was when we were entering Ballybofery. As we passed the sign warning drivers to reduce speed he pressed on the accelerator and we shot along the main street like an ancient runner making a final spurt for the tape.

Conveniently enough, the bus stopped outside a pub. The name was R. E. Doulan and Sons, and below that, Fine Wines and Brandies. Several men, most of them wearing cloth caps and smoking pipes, stood at the bar.

The whiskey wasn't Old Comber but it was pure *uisge beatha* to my aching body. I sat there for an hour, sipping on another three large ones and listening to the old boys talking about tractors, pigs, pigeons, silage, and plug tobacco. I was hoping they would talk about something less interesting so that I could dash out to the lavatory and not miss anything. Then they got onto 'the North' and I seized my chance.

To call it a lavatory was being charitable: it was nothing more than a drain with walls on three and a half sides and open to the sky. It's probable I would have been less charitable had it been raining.

I was returning along the alley and had almost reached the doorway leading to the bar when I heard a voice that stopped me dead.

'Where is he now then?' came the posh-Belfast accent of Portuguese Joe.

Quickly, I slipped past the open door, onto the street. I walked briskly away from the pub, turned a corner — and there was Peppar.

But again I was in luck: he was looking the other way. I ran back the way I had come. Portuguese Joe was still in the pub but liable to come out at any second. There was another alley to my left; I dashed into it. It was a long alley and immediately I began to seek cover before Peppar looked down and saw me. A few yards away light poured out from a doorway which seemed to be a side-entrance to a hall. I went in and closed the door.

It appeared to be a large dressing room. Several people were sitting on benches around the walls, holding guitars or reading sheets of paper. A small pudgy man came up to me and said loudly but pleasantly:

'Mr. Gilfurphy?' Before I could answer he continued: 'We'd almost given up on you, Mr. Gilfurphy, but I expect you were held up on the road. It's a long drive from Derry.' He rubbed his hands together and smiled. 'You know, you're the biggest name we've had in this hall since' — he paused and thought — 'since Ruby Murray; and that wasn't yesterday.' He looked around the room. 'Your instrument's in the car, is it?' Then added: 'Oh, by the way, my name's MacHussey.'

I decided to play along. 'No, it's not. It's broken. Fell down the stairs. That's why I'm late.'

He looked shocked, placed both hands on his cheeks, his wrists touching. 'Mr. Gilfurphy! What a terrible thing to happen. What — a — terrible — thing — to — happen.'

He stood gazing down at the floor for a while, muttering softly over and over again, 'Boys a boys a boys.' Then he looked up. 'Mr. Gilfurphy! We're in luck.' He placed one hand on his baldy head. 'Mrs. Degrassey — the doctor's wife you know — came down poorly last Sunday, just collapsed upon the stage, poor soul. Anyhow, she left her instrument here and knowing Mrs. Degrassey I'm sure she would have no objection to a man of your reputation making use of it. I'll get it now.'

At the door he turned and said: 'While it may not be up to your standards, Mr. Gilfurphy, I can definitely assure you of its character.'

I sat down on a bench and lit a cigarette. A prim young woman who was sitting next to me with a bunch of papers in her hand glanced up shyly. I smiled and gave a friendly shrug.

'The show must go on,' said Mr. MacHussey, striding towards me with a familiar case. I was relieved that Mr. Gilfurphy had turned out to be a violinist. I can play most instruments but I am at my best with a violin.

'The hall's packed to the very doors, to the very doors. This is most unusual.' He winked. 'And I think you're the reason for that, Mr.Gilfurphy. Even in this age of pop culture, Bach will draw them every time . . . On in twenty minutes?' He hurried away without waiting for an answer.

Curious about the other performers, I picked up the case and went along to the side of the stage. A sad-looking man of about fifty was singing in a flat doleful voice: 'Let's be merry, let's be gay.' It was evidently the contrast between the song's sentiment and the singer's delivery that was causing the giggling that rippled from the audience.

Suddenly, the man became angry. He stopped and asked a girl in the front row just what in hell she was laughing at. His question served only to increase the general merriment: the girl, now doubled-up, could only shake her head, and the rest of the audience, also giving full rein to the laughter they had so inadequately tried to stifle, roared and shrieked until the man looked ready to explode with rage.

'You're nothing but a bunch of ignorant gaunches!' he shouted and stomped off the stage.

The next act, a Browning-Barrett dialogue, was delayed for five minutes to give the house time to settle down. This modest interlude, however, turned out to be much too brief and the actors' romantic posturing was received in a very hilarious manner.

I was watching this when Mr. MacHussey came up and informed me that I was on next. 'You're the only performer who can prevent this concert from turning into a shambles,' he added in a serious tone.

After Browning and Barrett had walked off shaking their heads, Mr. MacHussey went onstage and introduced me as the highlight of the evening 'who will play a selection of pieces from that famous immortal, Johann Sebastian Bach.'

I was feeling good as I walked to the centre of the stage: I was still chuckling over the fate of the previous two acts and I was anything but sober. The audience had by this time fully composed itself and I noticed a trace of resentment on several faces, now that, apparently, the fun was over.

I cleared my throat. 'For my first piece this evening I would like to play my own interpretation' — I glanced at Mr. MacHussey standing in the wing; he smiled and nodded — 'of Bach's concerto entitled "How the Donnellys Crossed the Rhine".' There was a wave of puzzled muttering as I took up my stance, with several people already starting to titter.

I winked at the sea of faces and started into that very lively jig, "Red Campbell's Ball". Then as the audience roared with pleasure I made my foot-tapping way through "The Galway Jig", "The Kitchen Maid's Reel", "The Rakes of Athlone", "The Culshie Mucks' Feast", and by the time I got to "Holland's Wedding" there was a general state of devil-may-care revelry. People were shouting and dancing, and one or two were passing around bottles of booze. They were all having a marvellous time.

Except Mr. MacHussey. After recovering from his initial shock he started to call out, 'Mr. Gilfurphy will you get off the stage. Please get off the stage.' After fifteen minutes he was almost begging me to stop. But I just smiled and played on and on.

Finally, several men ran out from the wings and attempted to drag me off. A roar of protest came from the audience, and a crowd surged up onto the stage. I broke free, threw down the remains of Mrs. Degrassey's violin, and ran out through the dressing rooms into the alley. As I walked to the street I could tell by the sound of smashing glass and wood that a lively mêlée was in progress.

Keeping a watchful eye for Peppar and Portuguese Joe, I sauntered off in search of somewhere to sleep. I felt pleased that I had left my mark on Ballybofery.

Chapter 11

When rogues fall out

I knew I was taking a risk hitch-hiking, but it was all I could do. It was out of the question to take a bus — now that I knew Peppar was trailing me. Stealing a car would greatly increase my chances of being picked up by the police; and as a suspected killer that was the last thing I wanted.

I had taken two risks the day before and although they had worked out, I didn't feel like stretching my luck. The first one was taking a bus out of Dunglow. Nobody would have expected a man on the run to do that: it was too obvious. And that's why it worked; the obvious became the unexpected. The second risk was putting myself in the spotlight at the concert. The same principle was involved there. People expect a fugitive to be hiding — not making a spectacle of himself before a large crowd, a matter of yards away from his pursuers.

After the concert I came across a caravan parked on some waste ground on the outskirts of the town. Once again my heel gained me admittance and I had my best sleep in days, awaking shortly after ten o'clock.

I wasn't having much luck with my hitch-hiking. I had expected that a well-dressed man would have no trouble at all getting a lift, but the cars just kept on passing by. By noon I was hot, dusty and irritated. I sat down on a low wall to have a cigarette and had just flipped the butt away when I saw a white Jaguar approaching. Without much hope, I stuck out my thumb, then swore routinely as it went past. Wearily, I stood up and as I started to walk I noticed that the Jaguar was sitting about a hundred yards down the road. Then I heard the blare of its horn and I stepped up my pace. Somebody had finally stopped for me.

'Strabane any good to you?' asked the driver as I opened the door.

He let out the clutch and we moved off; his gear changes were rapid, barely noticeable, and within seconds we were purring along at about 60 mph. I settled back in the sumptuous seat and studied the driver. He was fiftyish, tall, with well-groomed grey hair; a long Roman nose dominated his elegant face; his suit looked like it came from a master tailor who took five fittings and sent out statements marked in guineas.

He said: 'It's quite obvious from your appearance that you're not an ordinary hitch-hiker. What has you tramping these dusty roads . . . trouble with your car?'

'Yes. It was stolen.'

He sighed in sympathy. 'How tiresome for you.' He paused as we overtook a Mini. 'That happened to me once . . . oh, about three years ago . . . got it back in the end, though.' He gave a short hard laugh. 'And I can tell you that the chappie who stole it didn't get off at all lightly, no, not by a long chalk.'

'Was it this car?'

'No, my other one.'

'What make?'

'Jaguar, also,' he said casually.

I looked out at the passing fields and saw myself in a white linen suit striding across a perfect lawn towards my other girlfriend standing in a white dress and floppy Ascot hat beside my other Jaguar, and we're going to my other villa . . .

'I have a feeling for these cars,' he said. 'They're like the animal — fast and sleek, they take you ahead of the pack.'

'They're conspicuous too. I mean, how was that chap who stole your Jag going to dispose of it. He'd have to sell it outside the country.'

'Oh, I think anything can be disposed of, Mr. Holland.'

It took two seconds for that to sink in, then my hands were hard against the dash, stopping my head from hitting the windscreen as he brought the car to a violent halt.

I jerked back in the seat, then went for my revolver.

'Hold it!'

I had almost made it. I glanced at the small gun in his hand then let my Chief's Special drop back into my pocket.

'These Baby Brownings are dainty little things,' he said, smiling. 'But they're more than adequate at this range.'

I heard a noise behind me. The driver shouted 'No!' and I looked round to see the sailor poised to bring a tyre-iron down upon my head.

'No, not yet,' the driver said calmly. 'We're going to give Holland a chance.'

I turned away from the sailor's hate-filled eyes,

feeling a little sick as I imagined the iron bar laying open my head.

The driver said: 'Put your hands behind your neck and —'

'So you're McKaine,' I said, grasping my burning neck.

His eyes flashed with anger. 'Who?'

'Don't come the old soldier with me, McKaine. It's no secret you're involved in this.' I turned and sneered at the sailor as I added: 'Sailor-boy here likes to shoot his mouth off.'

'That's a lie! It was Doreen.'

I sat back and looked at McKaine. 'The kid's better than a press release.'

There was a glimpse of the sailor's execution in McKaine's eyes as he stared past me. I said: 'That's why he was so eager to use the tyre-iron. He wanted to make sure I didn't talk. Maybe now he'll wait until he gets your say-so.'

'All right, you've had your fun,' McKaine snapped. He said to the sailor: 'No point in hanging around here. Get behind the wheel. I want to have a little chat with Holland about what he found on the island.'

He got out and stood at the door, pointing his Baby Browning at me. The sailor took his place and in two seconds McKaine was in the back seat. 'Let's go,' he said. 'Make a U-turn.'

We swung across the road, then there was a grinding noise as the sailor searched for reverse gear. McKaine shouted: 'Be more careful, you idiot!' But the grim-faced sailor paid no attention. He took the next bend fast, almost losing control as the car veered towards the ditch.

'Slow down!' shrieked McKaine.

The sailor's response was immediate. With an almost frightening surge of power the car reached 90 mph on the straight. The next bend, which had seemed so far away, loomed up within seconds. The sailor braked hard then fought the car round as we seemed certain to go off the road.

As I held on tight to the dash he completed the turn then roared up the next straight. I glanced back at McKaine. He looked anxious, but the gun was still levelled at my head. I was anxious too, even though I had planned to goad the sailor into driving in such an erratic way that we would go off the road. But this was more than I'd hoped for. The sailor had gone berserk. McKaine kept shouting at him to pull over, but this seemed only to increase his recklessness. He braked too late going into a right-hand bend; the car shot over to the wrong side of the road; he tried to regain control by straightening the wheels then accelerating. The car lurched out of the bend, still on the wrong side, and McKaine screamed as the parked car seemed to hurtle towards us.

Simultaneously the sailor braked and swung the wheel to the left. The parked car blurred, there was a crash as the back of the Jaguar struck metal, then my stomach came up to my mouth as the car overturned. With an explosion of sound the roof smashed against the ground. I almost lost consciousness as a massive jolt went through my body. Then a pandemonium of crashing noises and shocks as the car rolled into the ditch.

The next thing I knew I was lying below the dash with my hands over my face. I dragged myself back into the passenger seat and looked around. The car was sitting on its wheels, the sailor was slumped unconscious over the steering wheel, and his boss was face down in the back.

I staggered out and tugged open the back door. Grabbing McKaine by the feet, I pulled him out. His head banged against the ground but I'd no time to be gentle. I grasped him under the arms and dragged him about ten yards along the ditch. As I stumbled back for the sailor there was a noise like gushing steam and I threw myself to the ground. I lay there and waited, then the car exploded.

I crawled back to McKaine. He was still unconscious. I dragged him to a safer distance, then patted his clothing for weapons. I looked back at the burning car. There was a second, smaller explosion, then lots of dense smoke as the oil ignited. I said a prayer for the sailor.

A man was running towards me. I started to limp away but he came after me and put his hand on my shoulder. I shook him off and continued to walk as best I could. The man shouted after me but I kept on going.

Chapter 12

When rogues get rough

The next day, in the early afternoon, I was back in Belfast. Needless to say, I was very disappointed with the outcome of my expedition; but as my old unarmed-combat instructor used to say, I'm a great bouncer-back. I felt discouraged but not defeated.

Sitting on a bench in the G&R train and bus station, I tried to figure out my next move. It seemed like I'd been on the receiving end in this case for too long; it was about time, I decided, that I started hitting back. I thought of the old Bernard Holland and his no-nonsense ways. I remembered how things used to be. How men used to step aside with their eyes down when I approached, knowing that any back-talk or even a dirty look got them my fist in their mouth. How, as a contractor on the building sites in England, I'd line up the work-seeking Culshie Mucks against a ditch and go down the line, selecting and rejecting. 'Piss off,' I'd say to this one and that one, and then push them in the ditch if they answered back.

And how, with stengun in hand, I led my nerve-wracked men against the German-held farmhouses in France. There was nothing on Earth that could stop us as, howling like devils and scorning their fire, we ran at them, paralysing them with our terrible courage. A grenade and a stengun spray into each room, then on to the next farmhouse.

I remembered how, in Toronto, I battled Wellington Woodley for ten bloody rounds, six of them with my left ear hanging by a thread. He was a contender for the Empire title but he never fought again.

That was how it used to be. Before I let myself be pushed around by the authorities and my wife. Before I became a has-been. One of the old timers at boxing events who rise half out of their seats when acknowledged by the MC, clasping their hands above their heads in the veterans' salute, as the crowd applauds politely.

There was one drink left in the half-bottle of whiskey, so I drank it. I stamped out my cigarette then strode towards the Great Victoria Street entrance. People were entering the station to catch trains and buses for Dublin, Dunmurry, Newry, Banbridge, Dungannon and the rest. But they weren't going anywhere unless I let them. They had to get past me first, because I stood at the entrance and I was looking for people who had pushed me around.

Where's that thin-faced clerk from the labour exchange who kept refusing me money and saying I was unskilled? Then he tried to get me charged with disturbing the peace just because, sorely provoked, I made two V signs and shouted 'Up you, you effing bastards!' Where's that greasy manager who banned me from the Roxy cinema for shouting out? Where's that orange-peeling Mediterranean who blamed me for smashing up his cafe in Salthill? Where's Sergeant Murkley and his lawmongers? Where's Peppar now that I'm looking for him? Where's McKaine? Where's the Professor?

I must have stood there for at least five minutes before I decided to make myself less conspicuous. I still didn't know whether I was going to play dead or not, but I felt it advisable to keep my options open. I had been careless because I was angry. I had inspired myself too much. I pulled my hat down over my eyes and walked away.

The idea of setting up an H.Q. at Sleepy Sid's place came to me as I left the station. Looking across at Robinson's and the Crown, I remembered how we used to meet in one or the other of those pubs during the war.

His name derives from the time he was in North Africa with me. We were on a two-day reconnaissance patrol and at one point, when he was supposed to be keeping watch, I discovered him asleep in a sandbank. That lapse caused us to miss our rendezvous with the rest of the patrol, and as Sid and I tried to make our way back to camp we strayed a little off course. Then, rounding the top of a ridge, we received an unpleasant surprise in the shape of forty or fifty Italian soldiers who were resting at the bottom.

Nothing happened for about ten seconds: we just stared at them and they stared at us. Sid whispered, 'Looks like our war's over, pal.' I nodded once or twice, and at that point, to my surprise and relief, the Italians started to stand up with their hands over their heads. Before long we had formed them up into a squad, and it was one of my proudest moments when, to a reception of cheers and amazement, we entered the camp with the crestfallen prisoners, Sid calling the time and halting them before the company commander's tent. And then the expression on Major Teddington's large bespectacled face as I relayed the details of my latest initiative, excepting of course Sid's little snooze, and the major, with his pipe and baggy shorts, nodding a lot and saying it was a terrific piece of soldiering all right.

Apart from a few business links in the early sixties, Sid and I went our separate ways after the war; but we met occasionally on the street or in a pub, and each of us knew that the other was there should he be needed.

I called his number from a booth in Great Victoria Street. As I had expected, he was pleased to hear from me. Just give him enough time to slip out to the off-licence, he said, then dander on up. I didn't have far to go — he lived in a terraced house off the Grosvenor Road — so I set off at a slow pace, enjoying the sun.

Outside may be grime and broken glass, but Sid's house was his refuge and he did his best for it. There wasn't a trace of sophistication in anything that small living room held, but it was shiny and clean.

I put down my beer glass on the tiled hearth and lit a cigarette. 'What are you doing these days?'

In his new green blazer with boxing badge and a parting in his Brylcreemed hair almost as straight as the knife-edge crease in his grey flannel slacks, Sleepy Sid stood beside the bird cage, hands behind his back and at ease.

'I'm on the Liverpool boat nowadays. A wee man I drink with got me the job after I was laid off at the shipyard. Got in yesterday morning from the 'Pool and tonight I'll be going back again.'

'Sounds like something I would like. I bet you have a fair time in Liverpool.'

'Aw, you couldn't beat it. I work the First Class with a wee man from the Newtownards Road. Plenty of free feeds and drink and you're away from the rowdies. Then at the other side there's a club . . .'

We talked for a while about his new job and what I was doing — I didn't mention the case — then he remarked that he'd seen Gloria the day before.

'. . . there she was, full as a fool, linking this big fella up Royal Avenue and the two of them singing "She loves me, yea, yea".'

'What time was this?'

'Oh . . . about two o'clock.'

I got up, went to the window and parted the lace curtains. I didn't see anything in the street because I was walking away from a Jaguar and a man I called the sailor, and both were still burning at two o'clock.

'Another beer, Bern?'

I turned round. 'Sid, can I stay here for a few days?'

'Stay as long as you want.'

'What happened was —'

'It's not necessary,' he said, giving me a penetrating look.

He went out and there was the clink of beer bottles from the kitchen. I was glad I hadn't had to lie to him and I think he was glad too.

The next morning I did some serious thinking. It had been plain to me for some time that the document I'd taken from Dunslaney's papers had been part of a ruse to divert attention from where the bank money was hidden. There were two major suspects. Dunslaney was the obvious one, and it was to be hoped that his secret had not died with him; the other one was Faye.

My trip to Dunglow had accomplished two things. Firstly, I was now almost certain that Findargad was the general location: the gunman Peppar knocked out was not roaming around the island without a reason; nor, for that matter, was the major. Secondly, I now knew that my known rivals — Peppar and Portuguese Joe on one hand, and McKaine and his boys on the other — were no better informed than I was.

I had no clear idea why Dolan had been knocked off, but it seemed that whoever shot him was really after me. Realising that my days were numbered if I didn't defuse the situation, I decided to contact the man whom I suspected was behind it all — McKaine — and attempt to come to terms. Explain that he had nothing to fear from me and offer to co-operate with him in the search for the money.

First of all, I would suggest to him, we'd pay Miss Dunslaney a visit, perhaps lean on her a little, find out what she's playing at. Then we'd pull in PJ, duff him up a bit, get the word on Peppar; and then, after we'd taken care of the major, we'd send him back to British Intelligence as a warning to stay out of Belfast. Yes, and while we were taking care of people it would seem a shame to neglect Sergeant Murkley. And after that . . . why, even the Professor would not be safe from us. 'Open up! Inspector Wilkinson of Special Branch here!' Then we'd barge on in and give the Professor the worst thumping of the lot.

I reached for the phone. McKaine was in the office of his furniture business. As soon as he answered I slammed down the receiver. I didn't want a welcoming committee when I arrived.

The Targit Furniture Company occupied the ground floor of a tall shabby building in the east end. I opened a door that said OFFICE and went in. I was in a large room that held two wooden desks, a typewriter and two old filing cabinets. There was nobody there and according to the layer of dust on the furnishings nobody had been there for a while. At the other end of the room was a door; as I walked towards it the shape of a man moved across the frosted glass.

I didn't bother to knock. McKaine was sitting behind a large desk. Three heavies were sitting in a row along the wall. I didn't like it when two of them jumped to their feet and reached inside their coats. McKaine just gave an ugly smile and said:

'Talk of the devil.'

I said: 'It's time to talk, McKaine.'

McKaine said: 'Get him!'

I was already backing off. I slammed the door and stepped to one side. As the first man came out I booted him in the stomach; he yelled and fell back. That gave me enough time to run across the large room. I closed the door marked OFFICE behind me and instead of running out into the street I went along the corridor and up the stairs.

Four storeys later I was on the roof. I crouched down beside a boarded-up skylight to catch my breath. Then the roof-door was flung open and two of the heavies emerged with guns in their hands. Still crouching, I backed out of their line of vision; then I stood up and ran to the edge of the building. There was a low wall and beyond that, no more than four feet away, was the next building. I stepped up on the wall and jumped. I landed well, then ran to the roof-door and tugged, then pushed. It was locked.

I looked back. They were jumping across. I had no choice but to try for the next rooftop. Running low, I made it to the next wall, leaped up. A large gap yawned before me. I tried to stop, but I had too much momentum. My stomach heaved as I fell forward. I twisted and made a grab at the wall. My fingers scraped down the side of it, then a sharp silent scream as I started to fall.

My feet struck something hard, then my back. For a moment I was in the air again. Another slam against my back, this time much harder. Barely conscious, I lay still on the ground, looking through red flashes at a simmering brick wall and trying very hard to breathe.

But I knew there was no time to lose. Hurt as I was, I managed to stand up, holding on to the wall for support. I was in an alley. There was a car with its right fender against the wall. I could hear the engine running. I staggered over to it, opened the door and looked inside. The driver lay across the wheel; above him the roof had caved in. It seemed I had landed on top of him. I turned his head towards me. It was the heavy Peppar had overpowered on the island. He was still alive, but not by much. I switched off the engine, looked both ways down the alley, then picked up my hat and hobbled away.

My injuries had stiffened and after trudging up the narrow curved stairs I was in no shape to take off my hat, let alone my shoes. I just flopped onto Sid's single bed and started to unwrap the bottle. I even had trouble holding that up to my mouth; the whiskey ran down my chin onto my collar and I thought short bitter thoughts about Buck McKaine.

When I got around to Faye I didn't know what to think. She at least would be an easier proposition than McKaine. No rooftop chases or high-speed crashes with her. But I was still reluctant to contact Faye since that meant letting one more person know I was alive.

I had given some thought to the problem of pursuing my enquiries without making my presence generally known, and I felt that the whole thing was, more or less, in the hands of Fate. One unlucky encounter and the secret would be out.

But if I were to conduct the investigation properly,

I had to make myself known to certain people. I couldn't go flitting around like a spectral detective, appearing out of the void to demoralise my opponents with inane chuckling.

And so it is time for Bernard Holland to shed his ordinary identity and become . . . THE FEARLESS SHADOW. There he goes into the dark alley to concentrate on the mysterious brain waves taught to him by the Professor in the Liverpool pubs before the war. Soon his mind is throbbing with power. A quick drag on his Camel, then away, slinking softly down the street.

Looming suddenly before a man waiting for a bus, he fixes him with piercing eyes, urging him into a trance. 'You are now of the same thinking mind as me,' he drones. 'You will obey. You will destroy Sergeant Murkley and Portuguese Joe.' But the man doesn't obey. He hits THE FEARLESS SHADOW in the solar plexus and then walks off.

Something in me laughed at that. It might have been a part of my mind that didn't know I was in serious trouble, or knew and laughed anyway; the part that sniggers when people are telling me about their heart attacks or how the surgeon left his scissors in their belly. But I didn't see anything funny. I just got up, checked my Chief's Special, then started out for Faye's house. I was just a weary, unlaughing man entering the most crucial phase of the investigation.

Chapter 13
The brute and the temptress

As I passed the Roxy I noticed that *Lawrence of Arabia* was on for a full week: a film that in the ordinary course of events I would have gone to see. Being banned presented no problem, of course: two minutes putting on my false beard and nose would have taken care of that. However, I think it's only fair that I should be allowed to put the record straight regarding that ban.

The only reason I was shouting out that afternoon was to restore order. It's not often I have the chance to see *The Big Sleep* and *The Maltese Falcon,* and I became very annoyed with those students who laughed at and mimicked Humphrey Bogart each time he spoke. Then when I shouted at the students, the usherette had the audacity to shine her torch at me. She kept perfectly quiet while they were making all sorts of lewd comments during the first film. Yet as soon as I let fly a few remarks about students — just after *The Maltese Falcon* had started — she said 'I've warned you before,' and off she marched to find the manager.

I went quietly enough, almost with dignity, I would say, even though I was being subjected to derision from the students and remarks from the manager like, 'You should know better at your age, you know.' In fact, he didn't tell me I was banned until after I accidentally stepped back and drew my heel down his shin. I apologised profusely of course, but there was just no appeasing a man like that — plump rotten and miserable like everybody else in his family (the Sprattes who used to go around with a rag and bone cart) — and the curses he came out with were a complete disgrace, particularly so when one considers the obligations of his position and the fact that I must have been one of the Roxy's most long-standing patrons.

Past the cinema I turned south down a narrow sloping street lined with boarded-up shops and terraced houses. Even though I knew I was going to enjoy cutting up rough with that perfidious bitch, Faye, my showdown with her lay so heavy on my mind that I didn't realise there was a vehicle behind me until, hearing a sudden roar, I stopped and looked back.

There was just time to flatten myself against a doorway as the car bore down, missing me by inches. I started to run back up the street. The car screeched to a halt. Then the harsh tone of the engine as it moved in reverse.

As I approached the corner, a man appeared, moving slowly across the entrance to the street. Then he halted and turned to face me, his small crooked body framed against the sky. I stopped running. Behind me the car came to a halt. I waited, but no-one got out. I looked at the man, no more than ten feet away, and said:

'That gun's too big for you, Herman.'

He said nothing, just kept pointing the revolver at my chest. His eyes were wild, glaring, and the white cotton band drawn across his forehead seemed more macabre than ridiculous.

I held out my hand. 'You'd better give me the gun.'

He pulled the revolver back. I said softly: 'Come on, old son, that Japanese Warrior thing was only a game. You know that, don't you? Let's go and have a few drinks and you can tell me what happened.'

His expression didn't change. I still wasn't sure that he knew who I was. 'That's between me and . . .' He paused. The words had been measured out as if repeating a lesson. 'That's between me and the Japanese High Command,' he said.

'Get him away from the street!' said a voice from the car.

Herman didn't seem to understand. I said: 'I think she means we're too conspicuous here.' I had been inching forward and was now almost within rushing distance. As I steeled myself for the lunge, he stepped back and said: 'Turn round. Go back.'

In a nightmarish procession — the car crawling before me, Herman shuffling along behind — I walked slowly down the narrow street. In the car — a Rover, I now noticed — there were three men and a woman with a scarf over her head: McKaine's toughs and the blonde. The windows were down and two of the heavies were looking back at me.

I called over my shoulder: 'They're making a fool out of you, Herman.'

'You're the one who did that,' he shouted. 'You did that for years. You're the one who turned Frieda against me.'

'Nonsense.'

'Doreen knows you did. Doreen wants to be my

girlfriend and I won't let you drive her away too.'

I had already worked out that Doreen was the blonde. Herman was her zombie. She'd probably used drugs or hypnotism to soften him up; after that it was just a matter of manipulating his desires. Now the little man was a disposable killer; his usefulness ending as soon as he pulled that trigger. I said:

'She's using you for a fall-guy.'

'Do it now!' ordered the blonde.

The car stopped. Herman stopped. He raised his revolver and closed one eye. His hand shook violently. I felt very cold.

'They're going to drive off,' I said, 'and leave you for the cops —'

The blonde said sharply: 'Get on with it, Herman, or I won't be your girlfriend.'

But I had raised a doubt in his mind. He lowered the gun a little. He started to say, 'Are you —' Then the doors of the car opened and the three men got out. In one swoop I brought out my revolver and fired into the nearest one's chest. It must have been his neck that caught it, because his blood hit me in the face as I twisted slightly towards one of the others, aiming and squeezing the trigger almost simultaneously.

No response. I tried again. Nothing. It was jammed. I started to run. A bullet ricocheted off some brickwork in front of me. Swerving violently, I ran on. Bullets were smashing chunks out of the walls, whining deafeningly around me, filling the street with a cacophony of gunfire.

As I gained those vital yards the sound of firing seemed to become even louder. But I kept going, and as I neared the end of the street I felt for the first time that I had a chance. I swept round the corner, ducking low. Then an explosion of pain as I entered the void.

★ ★ ★ ★ ★ ★

I tried to open my eyes. A stream of blood was running over the left one, blocking my vision. I looked up one-eyed at a soldier. He extended his hand. I grabbed it, pulled myself upright then held on to a post for support. I took out my handkerchief and held it over the gash on my forehead.

'Run into the lamp-post, did you?' said the soldier. I shook my head. We walked down the centre of the street, now lined with soldiers. It was like ten minutes past high noon in Dodge: the day was still, a strong odour of gunfire hung in the air, and four men had bit the dust.

I stopped at the spot where Herman faced the sky. One arm was twisted under him; his right hand still clenched the revolver. He had been killed ten times over. Before the soldier could stop me, I bent over, wrenched the gun from Herman's grip and placed the muzzle to my nose. It hadn't been fired. Not even at me.

I looked down and said quietly: 'This was one game you weren't cut out for, Herman. Rest in peace.'

There was a tug on my arm and I started to walk. The soldier said he was taking me to the police barracks where his company had its H.Q. He thought that the police there would also be interested in questioning me. We climbed into a Land-Rover and moved away, leaving the rest of the patrol to guard the scene.

It was the first time I'd ever seen Sergeant Murkley smile.

'Now let's see what we have here,' he said as we faced each other in the 'interview room'. 'Involvement in a bank robbery, murder of Dolan, murder of a yet unidentified man, possession of an illegal weapon.' He held up four fingers in front of my face. 'That's four charges.'

'I'd like to —'

'Not yet, Bernard. Not yet. Time for that later.' He smiled again. 'You don't mind me calling you Bernard, do you? After all, we have known each other for a long time.' He leant back in his chair and lit a cigarette. I could have done with one myself.

'Cigarette, Bernard?' I shook my head. 'You know,' he said, 'all this even makes up for the disappointment I had when I found out you weren't dead after all.'

'You're sick, you know that? The city's full of killers and bombers, yet you're obsessed with persecuting a relatively innocuous —'

'Bernard! Didn't I tell you once before not to fancy-pants me? Relatively innocuous indeed. Now how do you expect a poor police sergeant to know what the like of that means?' Smiling viciously, he leant forward and whispered: 'But I do know how to give you a bloody good hiding.'

Seconds later a constable entered. Murkley scowled as the young cop whispered in his ear; then they both went out. A large man in plain clothes came in.

'All right, Holland. Let's start at the beginning.'

'Who are you?'

'Never you mind who I am. I want to know why you went to the island.'

So for the next thirty minutes I trotted out my detailed non-incriminating version of the truth. The large man didn't seem to be too impressed by my assertion that I was, in a manner of speaking, acting on behalf of British Intelligence.

'You make Peppar sound like a bloody sheriff,' he snorted. 'Deputising left and right as soon as the first outlaw waltzes up to the cabin.'

I was in no mood for sarcasm. 'He was doing a sight more than waltzing, I can tell you. And I'm sure Major Peppar will inform you of how I —'

'I know what Peppar will inform me.' He looked at his watch then started to collect his papers. 'You're free to go.'

'You mean? . . .' This came as such a surprise to me that I felt a strange impulse to protest. Surely they were not going to dismiss so casually a man with four major charges to his name.

'Holland, I said you're free to go.'

'All right, I heard you.' I stood up and went to the door.

'Oh, Holland.'

I turned. There was the glimmer of a smirk on his face as he said:

'I think you should get your head seen to.'

At least the lights were still on in Faye's house. I had almost staggered the last part of the way after my marching gave out. A staggering bloody-faced man who once thought it was merely a matter of taking a spin out to the west coast and digging a hole. I rang the bell.

The door opened to the extent of a thick brass chain. 'Bernie? . . . But I thought . . .'

'We don't have to talk on the doorstep, do we?'

'No, of course. Wait a second.'

I followed her in, then collapsed on the couch. When I opened my eyes she was standing in front of me, holding out a glass of whiskey.

'Well?' she said, and sat down beside me.

'Well what?'

'Oh, Bernie.' Her sigh was an expression of either exasperation or passion: I was too punchy to determine which. But knowing her, I assumed the former.

'Sorry, Faye, I'm not thinking too clearly. These past few days have been sheer hell for me. I've been shot at, hunted like a wild animal, virtually thrown from a high roof, framed for two murders and a bank robbery . . .'

'Poor dear, of course you have.' As she placed her hand on my forehead the earthy smell of her armpit was so stimulating that I could barely restrain myself from grabbing her. I looked longingly at her dark-tinted nylons and the shape of her black bra through the thin silk blouse.

'I didn't know what to do when you failed to come back,' she said. 'Then somebody told me you'd been killed. I just couldn't believe it. There I was, all on my own with that awful Herman —'

'He's been shot.'

'Really?'

'Dead as a doornail. Poor little bugger. Got in with the wrong crowd this time, that's for sure.'

'I think,' she said, 'you'd better tell me what happened.'

So I did. With one important exception, I told her exactly how everything happened. It was part of the plan.

'Really, Bernie, I think you should have taken me into your confidence before now.'

'I had my reasons.'

'Obviously . . . I think I'm going to have a very large drink.'

She brought me another one too. It tasted okay, but when I stood up my face hit the carpet. Then the ceiling came down.

Belfast is like a rat being shaken by a terrier. Even the stars vibrate as the storm rages and bangs and beats. A sea of badwater that runs as deep as we are human surges and eddies in the black plugged mind of the city. Lamp-posts bounce along the streets, leaving behind puddles of yellow light. I run for cover past twisted, staggering houses and pubs of brown glass. The Strangler's Arms reach out as I pass. 'Open my doors tonight,' it calls. 'My warm tables are full of surprise.' A tank rumbles behind me and I see Portuguese Joe in the turret. He looks at me through binoculars then shouts down orders to Sergeant Murkley. The large gun pivots as I run down towards the sea. Faye's there with a short spear, riding a dolphin till its heart bursts. The blast lifts me through the air. I'm floating over the city and over the sea.

Now I'm walking along the harbour with newspapers under my arm. All is quiet and sunny. A woman has a copy of *Ulysses* in her hand. A man is picking up a dead seagull.

I was too groggy to wonder why I couldn't move. Faye appeared for a few moments, left in a blur, then reformed. By this time I had the feeling my arms were holding me back. Maybe I was handcuffed to the chair. I cleared my throat.

'What . . . what did you put in the drink?'

She was sitting on the couch, smoking a cigarette and looking at me with cool made-up eyes. She said:

'Believe it or not, mastermind, I hadn't planned it this way. But then I became so tired of waiting that I decided the direct approach might be best after all.'

'You have the real map.'

'Yes. But the aggravating thing was I didn't know what district it applied to. I needed somebody to find that out for me — that's why I was pleased when you came along, looking for your wife's insurance papers or whatever.' She sipped from a glass of wine. 'Of course, at that time I didn't know you were a bungler.'

'Don't kid yourself. I've suspected you for a long time.'

'Not that I wanted someone bright enough to see what was happening, but after a while I had serious doubts that you would accomplish anything at all – apart, of course, from almost getting killed on several occasions. However, it seems that you did stumble on something after all. Sheer luck, most probably.'

'What happens if I don't tell you?'

She gave a short laugh. 'Don't underestimate me, Holland. You'll talk all right.'

'What happens after I tell you?'

'You're coming with me. I have to be sure you've told me the truth.' Suddenly she was pointing a revolver at my chest. 'And this is to keep you in line.'

I decided she wouldn't need that until we'd dug up the money. That's when we'd stop being valuable to each other. That's when my plan would enter its crucial – and perhaps bloody – final stage. Yes, I was playing her along. I really had suspected her for a long time. She was the only one left who could have had the real map.

'When are we leaving?' I asked.

'Right after you've told me,' she said, and stood up. She came over to me slowly, smiling. Almost sensually, she stroked my chin, making noises with the bristles. 'It's morning – or haven't you noticed?'

Chapter 14
A villain's put to the question

The Professor raised his hat. 'I really must compliment you on your initiative, my dear Faye. A remarkable performance by any standard. Well done.' He allowed himself a thin smile of triumph, then his long aquiline face was once more impassive. 'Not that I don't appreciate *your* little contribution, Bernard. A trifle ill-starred at times, perhaps, but then that is your way. On the whole, I would say, you have been useful. Now, put down the spade and bring that container to me.'

I placed the metal box on the ground in front of him, then stepped back. The Professor nodded at a short bulky man wearing sunglasses with mirror lenses and said:

'I should tell you that Albert wants to fire his shotgun at you both.' He sighed as if considering the whimsical notions of a small boy with a pop-gun. Albert made a little shuffling movement. 'Yes, I do believe he's becoming quite frustrated . . . To be fair to him, though, it has been rather a long time since I've allowed him to fire it. But then I ask myself: would it be inappropriate in the present situation for him to do that? . . . Albert, would it be inappropriate?'

'No, Professor.'

'Bernard?'

'Very much so, Professor.'

'Faye?'

She continued to stare at the ground. 'Faye?' he repeated politely, still, as it were, the gracious academic examining a case-study in anthropology with a slightly backward student. A student, moreover, who not only refuses to accept the relevance of the topic to her own situation but in certain aspects of her behaviour, such as keeping on her overcoat in the classroom, displays an attitude which the Professor would find irritating were he not still beholden to her for an earlier service; a service which, notwithstanding the fact that it was performed only unwittingly on his behalf, the Professor deemed sufficiently valuable to allow as an important consideration in the matter of accommodating the impulses of the conscientious but even more backward Albert.

It was perhaps this aspect of the situation that Faye contemplated as she worried a party of ants with the toe of her muddy boot. Then, with an expression that reminded me of the girl whose pleasure it was to kick doors, she delivered with her heel several swingeing blows to the dispersing insects and said:

'Go fuck yourself.'

Albert made another little shuffle. I swore under my breath. The Professor, however, did not seem at all displeased. 'My dear girl,' he said, 'that really was worth waiting for. You know, when one's associates are as obsequious as mine it can be quite refreshing to be spoken to like that. And how perceptive of you too. Yes, as you have no doubt realised, you will be accompanying me when I leave. It really would be a sin to waste something as beautiful as yourself.'

That line of reasoning, I realised with increasing consternation, obviously did not apply to me. It would have been difficult to imagine what use the Professor could make of my own scarred and somewhat elderly body.

'And as for you, Bernard, I have decided to let you go.' He nodded to confirm his decision then continued: 'Because when it comes down to the nitty gritty of this matter you really know very little at all. And the smattering you do know — well, let's just say that I am not averse to you airing it abroad. As doubtless you will, in a typically exaggerated form, the moment you get a drink in your hand.

'By the way, Bernard — and this may strike you as being irritatingly pious — but every report I have received on you has made mention of your excessive drinking. Perhaps you would be more successful if you eased off in that direction.'

The Professor certainly likes to rub it in, I thought. And no, Professor, there is no aspect of you that I would regard as even remotely pious.

He opened the metal box, fondled the bundles of notes, then replaced them in the wrapping. He said softly, as if to himself: 'Not enough here to justify killing Holland anyway.' Then, louder:

'Now really, I simply can not stand around here chatting all day . . . Bernard: time for you to leave us. You will find that your little boat is inoperable. By the time you have repaired it — assuming of course that you can — we will be long gone.'

I said: 'Can I have her car keys?'

The Professor permitted himself another smile. 'We are being practical, aren't we? But yes, of course. The lady won't be needing them. Albert will get them for you.'

For the last time I gazed upon Faye's superb body, particularly fetching in tight faded blue jeans and clinging sweat-soaked teeshirt; almost shuddering as I contemplated her fate as a prisoner of the Professor. After her will had been sapped with beatings and drugs, she would be kept in bondage as his sex-slave until her beauty faded or, more likely, until she no longer amused him. Her last pathetic years would be spent as a zombie in one of his overseas brothels.

I heard the Professor say: 'Au revoir, old chap. Look after yourself.' Then I picked up my hat and walked away.

I think that for once in my life I had been glad to see the Professor. Well, almost glad: when he and that Tonton Macoute stepped out of the bushes I was afraid they were going to kill us on the spot. That fear, however, was easier to bear than the stark reality of Faye raising the revolver and saying, 'Goodbye, Holland.'

I *had* underestimated her. It was not, as I had thought, simply a matter of overpowering her after I had dug up the money. Admittedly, I didn't think it would be easy, but I thought I could do it. As it turned out, she had been very cautious right from the moment we left her house. She didn't even bring the map with her; it was all in her head. All the time I was digging she stood about ten feet away, gazing at me as if deciding where the bullet was going to go. I would have rushed her, of course — I was on the point of doing that when the Professor arrived — but I'm sure she must have been expecting such a last-second effort.

The Professor was quite correct when he said the

boat was inoperable. Why he had taken the trouble to pull the engine apart, I didn't know. There are much quicker ways to disable a boat. However, I supposed it was one of the Professor's quirks. He wanted to think of me sitting on a stony beach trying to re-assemble an engine without any tools and all the while it's getting darker and darker. As if I didn't have enough troubles.

It was after eleven o'clock when I made it into Dunglow harbour. I tied up the boat then set off to where we had parked her blue Cortina. Needless to say, I was very tired, but I knew that sleep would not come to me this night. I decided to drive back to Belfast and reconsider the situation.

I parked the car in the street outside Sid's house. There was no sign of Sid. I spent a long time climbing the stairs to the bedroom, then I rewarded myself with a deep slug of whiskey. That gave me enough strength to undress and walk all the way to the bathroom. After I turned on the taps for a bath I let myself have another slug. By the time I had a shave and a long soak I was feeling good. I ate a tin of stew in the kitchen. It tasted just like tinned stew but it stopped me feeling hungry. I went to sleep on the sofa.

When I woke up, the loud clock on the mantlepiece said 9:25 a.m. Sunlight was streaming into the living room, brightening the already bright colours of the furniture and enhancing the gleam of the polished sideboard. It showed up a little dust too, but even that looked polished and in its place. There were a couple of sparrows chirping on the window sill. I listened to them for a while, then got up and switched on the radio. The announcer said it was going to be a fine day, and I thought that it probably would be for all sorts of people around the city. Maybe even for me. But it wasn't going to be a fine day for the man I was calling on next. He didn't know it yet, but the next stage of my plan meant fear and suffering for Portuguese Joe.

Lamia Road is lined with dying trees, old cars, and large oil stains where old cars have been. The houses are big, dull and dirty. Those in which the upstairs blinds are always down are the massage parlours, where posters of fantasy women look down upon sparse shabby furniture, overflowing ashtrays, and fireplaces full of used tissues.

There are also several rooming houses on Lamia Road. Sad places haunted by quiet, shuffling men seldom noticed by the other roomers: threadbare wandering people, down at heel ex-prisoners, alcoholics, and the fly boys who seem continually in transit between the bookie's, the pub and the billiard hall.

Number sixty-six was no dirtier than any of the other buildings. There was nothing on the walls or in the hall that a water-cannon couldn't shift. I climbed two flights of narrow stairs to the top floor, then walked quietly to a door at the end of the landing. Placing my ear against it I heard a noise like a man choking. There was only one person I knew who laughed like that. I banged on the door. I listened. Then I banged again. I shouted:

'Portuguese Joe, you'd better open this door.'

There was the sound of a bolt being drawn back, then the door opened an inch. I pushed it hard; it hit something and stopped. I pushed it again. This time I met with no resistance.

Portuguese Joe was staggering back, holding his forehead and looking badly scared.

'Didn't even have the sense to move,' I said, glancing around. 'Anybody in the bedroom?'

Joe attempted a recovery. 'Bernard, you have no right —' Then, seeing the look in my eyes, he relented.

'Just a friend in there,' he said.

I pushed him into the bedroom. A black-haired woman of about fifty sat on the bed. She was wearing a green dress and one nylon. Her nose was too large but she was fairly attractive in a ripe sort of way. She seemed resentful of my intrusion. Joe decided to protest again.

'Now, look here —'

'Don't get excited,' I told him. 'You and I are just going to clear up a few points, that's all.' I said to the woman: 'You can stay here till I leave. I won't be long.' I pushed Joe out of the bedroom and closed the door after me.

He went wearily over to the latticed window, looked out, then sat down in one of the two shabby over-stuffed armchairs. I sat opposite him, snapped on a large forties-type radio that was on the floor beneath the window, and said:

'You've got some explaining to do.'

He put a match to his cigarette, exhaling slowly, looking at me through narrowed eyes. There was a red mark on his perspiring forehead where the door had hit him. He was wearing black trousers and a blue striped shirt with the collar removed. A female blues singer was moaning something about a honey bee. The woman in the bedroom had opened the door about an inch; but there was nothing for either of us to hear except the blues singer and the sound of Portuguese Joe's breathing. Then:

'What do you mean I've got some explaining to do?'

I got up slowly, went over to the bedroom door, closed it sharply, then came back and slapped him very hard across the ear. His mouth opened in a long silent cry and tears or perspiration ran down his cheeks onto his neck.

I said: 'If I clout you with both hands at once the sudden air-compression will burst your eardrums.'

He gave one quiet sob then started to get up. I pushed him down, bent over so that my face was close to his, and said, almost hissing:

'None of us is going to come out of this business smelling of roses. None of us is going to be proud of himself — not for what he did or the way he did it. None of us has been all that bright. But some have been more stupid than others — real stupid, pathetically stupid — and they're the ones that copped it.

'The bloody thing's been a three-ringed circus from the word go — and you and I are the only fools who haven't got themselves wiped out yet. I'm still around because I'm a walking miracle. I'm probably the most shot-at man in the history of this city, and if that's not enough, I've been in a high-speed car crash and I've fallen off a roof. Now I'm here to tell you it's your turn.

'It's your turn because you lied to me, you tried to make me a dupe, you incited Peppar to beat me up, perhaps kill me. That's probably not all you did but it's all I know about at the moment. And now you have the fucking audacity to sit there and say "What do you mean I've got some explaining to do?"'

I sat down again, pulled out my pack of Camels and lit up at the second attempt. I was angrier than I thought. There was just no way out of this for Portuguese Joe unless he told me the truth.

'And consider yourself lucky you're getting this chance,' I added. 'Two other smart-Alecks who thought they'd try their hand at double-crossing me are now very much kaput. So you'd better tell it good. Right from the beginning.'

'What do you mean "from the beginning"?' he said.

I sighed. 'Joe,' I said, 'for a man who supposedly lives by his wits you are remarkably thick at times. Have I or have I not impressed upon you my dislike of this "what do you mean" business?'

'Yes, you have.'

'Good. I rather thought I had. Now you just start at what you think is the beginning. When you see me getting up from this chair you'll know you've left something out. There'll be at least five seconds to remember what it is before I clout you. Is that clear?'

'Graphically so.'

As it turned out, he was more than anxious that I should remain seated throughout his miserable story. It had been as I'd supposed: Portuguese Joe was a police informer. Four years earlier a deal had been made when they caught him trying to cash stolen travellers' cheques. After that he'd meet his detective on bridges, in parks, give him the whisper on who was suddenly flashing rolls of money, what was being said on the streets, in the bars, and so on. (As if it somehow lessened the stigma attached to being a nark, he emphasised that he did not stop committing crimes himself.)

Then, over a year ago, he was approached by British Intelligence in the person of Major Peppar. The Englishman wanted to plant him in a revolutionary group called the Black Ring, which was recruiting in Belfast. Joe adamantly refused, stating that he would prefer to go inside. The compromise was that Joe would make enquiries regarding several bank robberies which Peppar believed to be the work of that group.

Marcus Dunslaney — a disaffected communist who became an officer in Black Ring — was his only lead. Joe followed him to Dunglow, where he witnessed an attempt on Dunslaney's life. What struck him as peculiar was the risk Marcus took in ensuring that a letter was posted. After that it was all guess work on Joe's part. He said he knew nothing of McKaine or the sailor.

Joe watched me anxiously as I drummed my fingers on the arm of the chair. An unspoken question hung in the air between us: What did I propose to do next?

'What have you got to drink?' I said.

'Brandy . . . '

'That'll do. Fetch the bottle and two glasses.'

As he opened the doors of a battered oak cabinet I could see an array of spirits, liqueurs, wines, even a soda syphon. He came back with an almost full bottle and the glasses. I now knew why he had been so quick to offer brandy.

'That's Australian stuff,' I said.

He put his head to one side and looked down earnestly at the bottle on the coffee table. 'So it is,' he said as if I had just informed him that his finger was dripping blood onto the carpet. 'I assure you, Bernard, it was no intention of mine to pass off cheap brandy upon a man with your . . . '

'Knowledge of drinking?'

' . . . expertise.'

'That's all right,' I said lightly. 'There's nothing wrong with a drop of down-under.'

He sighed and reached for the bottle. 'In that case, I shall pour with a generous hand.'

'Put it down,' I said.

He looked puzzled. 'What do you mean?' Then, hastening to wave away the forbidden words: 'I mean, I thought you wanted —'

'Come now, Joe. You don't really think I'd drink with a stool pigeon, do you?'

He pulled out his handkerchief and dabbed nervously at his face. 'I don't understand.'

'Yes, you do. I want you out of here in two minutes. Go for a walk, meet your copper friend, do what the hell you want, but get out of here.'

'You don't mean . . . ?'

'Yes. Now scoot.'

His mouth opened to protest, made a soft moaning

noise, and slowly closed. He stared at the carpet for a few seconds, then turned towards the door. I said:

'You know how things are, don't you, Joe? I wouldn't want you to be doing anything foolish.'

He paused with his hand on the knob. 'Yes, I know how things are.'

I moved up behind him and said softly: 'Good. Now who is that woman in there? Is she a whore?'

'No, she's a . . .'

'Out with it. I can find out from her.'

Joe stared at the door, his hand still on the knob. A long ten seconds went by. I jabbed him over the right kidney, not hard, just enough to remind him how things were. He grunted, then said:

'She's a woman I know something about.'

'What?'

'Conviction for fraud in England.'

I felt like hitting him again but I didn't. I said tightly: 'From now on you leave her alone. Understand?'

He nodded. I went over to the coffee table and poured a drink. It tasted all right. When I looked round, the door was closed and Portuguese Joe had gone.

Carrying the bottle and the glasses, I walked over to the bedroom. As I opened the door the woman sat up and passed her hands over her cheeks. I poured her a drink then sat down beside her.

'He won't trouble you any more,' I said. 'I've warned him off.'

She drank half of the brandy then took a tiny embroidered handkerchief from her pocket and dabbed at her eyes. She said in a small voice:

'Who are you?'

'Never you mind who I am,' I said gently, 'but what I told you is true.'

She looked at me for several seconds, her eyes large and doubting, then her hands went up to her face and she started to sob.

Chapter 15

The detective's last argument

The woman didn't care for a lift home. I followed her down the stairs and then stood watching as she walked quickly away, her high heels tapping on the cracked pavement. She was a nice woman with a tiny voice who had broken the law and paid for it time after time in that small damp bedroom at the top of number sixty-six Lamia Road.

Perhaps it had been none of my business to get involved in Joe's private dealings, but I had acted upon man's primal urge to protect women, particularly victims, and now I felt just a little more satisfied with myself. I got into Faye's Cortina, put down the visor against the harsh, reflecting sunlight, then drove off in the direction of my house.

I called the number from the phone box at the end of

the street, letting it ring fifteen times before replacing the receiver. I had a clear field. After entering the house I stood silent for a few moments, listening for movement inside. There was just the hum of the refrigerator motor and beyond that the faint sound of sparrows chirping.

I went into the living room, to the shelves of books beside my armchair. They didn't seem as packed as before but I had no time now to track down missing books. At one time I had a sign up: Please Do Not Ask for the Loan of Books as a Refusal often Offends; but the wife said it was ridiculous and took it down. As she did my earlier sign: Please Note that Bernard Holland Does Not Run a Taxi Service, which was for the benefit of those car-less neighbours and relatives (mostly Canadian) who expected to be taken places.

It was all right for the wife to say that my signs were ridiculous — and to a certain extent they were — but they weren't her books that were being taken away and never returned, and she wasn't the one who had to get up at the crack of dawn to drive people to the airport.

Next to the shelves was a small locked cabinet where I kept some of my papers. I had been meaning to transfer these to the office but hadn't got round to it. Not that it mattered all that much: they weren't my confidential papers, and as I had installed a heavy-duty lock on the cabinet they were reasonably safe there. I opened it and began to sort through a bundle of letters arranged very roughly in chronological order. I soon found what I wanted; it was a report from Sleepy Sid dated September 1960:

'. . . I'm still adding to the PLAN. I think we'd be fools not to try it because it could mean the BIG TIME. Try and find some agents over there who are of the same mind as us, only some of them will be fall guys in case anything goes wrong or comes out into the limelight. No one (not even his home) has heard as yet from the

Professor. I wouldn't be surprised or alarmed to hear he's on the streets, taking an odd shot, or doing magic tricks in dives. I heard in O'Brians he was in trouble down the Free State and was fined a lot of dough but its not like him to get caught and I think they were talking about Billies brother who was also in Liverpool.

'But who could have forseen (and I must confess that you did) that the Professor would double cross. Its a nice way to be paid for your pains. Call as soon as you arrive back and we'll have a few shots of "Mundies Wine" and if you meet up with the Professor don't be shy, because he's on dangerous ground . . .'

I put this letter back then pulled out a thick notebook. Using the index — which I'd long since failed to update — I found two entries devoted to the Professor and British Intelligence. The first one went back to the early days of the war. I was in the SAS then; indeed, I just wasn't in it — in a manner of speaking, I *was* it. At that time it existed only on paper, a ruse to confuse the enemy; and British Intelligence, recognising my abilities for a special assignment of this nature, had me knocking around London in uniform with SAS flashes on.

One day, when having lunch at the Cafe Royal, I heard this commanding voice discoursing upon hypnotism. Turning round I saw the Professor sitting with a beautiful and apparently wealthy woman. I knew at once I'd made a mistake coming out that day as a mere captain; but, nothing ventured, nothing gained, I moved across to their table, ostensibly to discuss something with the Professor.

As it turned out, I didn't make much headway with the woman, even though she was as gullible as she was lovely. I didn't know where to look when she cried 'How marvellous, darling!' after he claimed to have hypnotised Mesmer himself. At that moment I couldn't think of anything to top that — well, I was quite young — and the

Professor proceeded to dominate the conversation.

They went out together, arm in arm, and it wasn't until I was about to leave that I discovered they had left me their bill. Luckily, I could afford the sizeable amount they had run up. What with the black market and getting things on credit by exploiting my rank of major (nominal), I was doing very nicely until Stirling went and spoilt it all by forming the real SAS.

That brought back memories, but it was the second entry that held my interest. I read it carefully, then re-read it. I put the notebook back and took out an imitation Saturday Night Special I'd bought by mail order in Canada. I leered at the dummy revolver for a while, handling it and getting the feel of it again. I put it in my jacket pocket, then drew it out in a fast, practised sweep, placing the muzzle against the spine of *Ulyssean Man.* I whispered, 'This is it, bub, spill your guts or fade.'

As I practised my crouch shot, there was the sound of a car stopping outside. I went quickly to the window, looked through the venetian blinds. It was the red Mini of the prison warder next door. I watched as he walked up the path, grim profile, looking straight ahead. A sour, silent man; ex-Hong Kong Police — or so he'd said on one of the few occasions we'd talked, before he decided he disliked me.

Time to get out of here. I locked the cabinet then glanced around for any little thing that might betray my visit. Everything was just as she liked it. No ash in the ashtray, no books on the floor, no husbands who drink beer and whiskey and who smoke pipes whch stain the ceiling and leave burns on their shirts, no husbands who just want to go to hell in their own way, too selfish to devote their lives to headachy, grasping wives, neat hatbox houses, and boring, killing jobs from which they get to spend one-twentieth of their salaries.

Not that I was in a philosophic frame of mind as I drove towards the Targit Furniture Company. There is nothing less abstract than a desperate man determined to bring a critical affair to a sudden conclusion — one way or the other.

I was both surprised and relieved to find McKaine's Jaguar in the small carpark at the back of the building. This time, however, I had no intention of rushing in. I stepped back into the shadows and waited.

There were moments during the next hour when I felt like taking a chance with a direct assault — in my keyed-up state the inaction was almost unbearable — but I managed to restrain myself by thinking of what happened the last time. Then, just after six o'clock, my patience was rewarded. There was the sound of a door closing, then McKaine appeared, striding towards his car, and — my luck was still with me — he was alone.

As he placed the key in the lock I started to move, quickly and silently. He was standing with the door open when I came up behind him. Pressing my Saturday Night Special into his back, I pushed him into the driver's seat, at the same time releasing the catch on the rear door. I climbed in and jabbing the revolver into his cheek, growled: 'Get moving.'

He looked back with an expression of both alarm and disbelief. I jabbed him again. 'Move. Now!'

'For God's sake, Holland,' he cried.

'Get this car moving!'

He glanced at the door to his offices. 'You're only making it worse for yourself —'

'You'd be dead before they can reach me. Keep your hands away from your pockets. Get moving, I said.'

'You must realise —' The blade of my flick-knife across his neck discouraged him from saying any more. As I brought it back I could see a thin red line, and in his eyes a sudden burgeoning of fear.

'All right,' he said hoarsely, and turned the ignition.

For a few minutes we headed east along residential streets. Entering a quiet stretch adjacent to a park, I told him to pull over.

'So you're the Professor's brother in law, eh, McKaine?' I said as we sat with the engine running.

He just stared ahead, his hands on the wheel. I nodded wearily as if to confirm my earlier expectation that he'd be a hard one to crack. 'Answer me,' I shouted in his ear.

'I'm sorry, but I don't know what you're talking about.'

'Don't you? I think you do. I think you also know where the money is.'

'I did not find the money.'

We could go on all day at this rate. Grabbing his hair, I made a long superficial cut down the back of his ear. He yelped in pain and brought his hands up to protect himself.

'Put them down,' I shouted, slashing at his hands.

'All right, Holland! You win.'

I stopped slashing and slid across the seat, away from him. 'Get moving,' I said. 'You can talk on the way.'

As we drove along the coast road I asked him for details of his operations, but he refused to say anything on that matter. I was getting the money, he said, and that was all. In a way I was glad he refused: the intensity of the subsequent manhunt, with me as the quarry, would be great enough without the pressing requirement of silencing a man who knew far too much. But curiosity often overcomes prudence.

We stopped at a house overlooking the sea. The windows were boarded up and the small garden adjacent to the road was overgrown with weeds. It had at one time, I thought, been a guest-house of sorts. Indeed, I seemed to remember staying there myself, along with a now faceless girlfriend, back in the fifties.

As he unlocked the front door I warned him that if this were a trap I would shoot him without hesitation. He said nothing, just pushed open the door and preceded me inside. I followed him closely down the hall into a dark, cobwebbed room that had once been the kitchen.

'Over here,' he grunted, stepping carefully towards the range. 'I'll need some light.'

I stood behind him, holding my lighter to one side, and watched as he used a penknife to remove several bricks from the wall. Then he heaved out a large metal box, eased it to the floor, and stood there in the flickering light, looking at me with no particular expression.

'Open it,' I said.

He bent over, and less than a minute later I was gazing at bundles of ten- and twenty-pound notes wrapped in heavy plastic being set on the floor. I had gone through sheer hell for these, but there was little exultation: just a feeling of rage that it had cost so much. I looked at McKaine, no longer the feared adversary, and with a snarl of contempt brought the revolver down hard on the side of his head. As his hand jerked out for the wall, his legs gave way; his knees hit the floor; then, after a long sigh, so did his face.

'Now you know your victims can strike back,' I said harshly as he began to stir. 'Yes, that's right. Me, Bernard Holland, I've struck back. And I've done it for everybody who's been hurt by you and the Professor. All the people, dead or alive . . .'

I gave it up. My head was throbbing and I just wanted to get out of there. He probably couldn't hear me anyway. I replaced the bundles in the box then carried it out to the car. It seemed somehow fitting that I should be returning to Belfast in a Jaguar.

Chapter 16
Imitation Artillery

'What's taking you across the water?' asked Sid, combing his hair at the mirror above the fireplace. The hand-painted red roses around the edges of the frameless glass gave him the appearance of a garlanded racing driver; even the cigarette dangling from his lips did not seem out of place.

'Just business, Sid. Look, I was wondering . . .' This was the tricky part. Somehow, I had to get £120,000 in notes out of the country, past the security personnel who examined the contents of each item of luggage; and to this end I was banking on Sid's willing, but unwitting, assistance.

'. . . I have a suitcase in the hall which I don't want checked as I go aboard. I was wondering if you could take it on for me.'

He placed his comb on the mantlepiece and turned to face me. 'Do you know what you're asking?'

'There's nothing illegal in that suitcase. No guns, explosives or drugs. It's just that I would be embarrassed if anyone were to look through it, that's all.'

'Well, I don't know, Bern . . . He stared at the carpet for a good ten seconds, then let out a deep breath. 'All right . . . But I don't like it.'

'Good man.' I took out my wallet, counted out six fivers and reached them to him.

'There's no need for that,' he said, shaking his head. I pushed them down the neck of his shirt, then went into the kitchen for a beer.

At Liverpool's Lime Street Station I boarded the London train. My earlier fears that I might be followed had been somewhat appeased by the fact that I had managed to get as far as this. If they were going to apprehend me now, I felt, they would almost certainly have to do so before I reached London, for once I went to ground in that city I was virtually immune from capture.

I had decided before leaving Sid's house not to make use of my disguises. My feeling was that since I had appeared so often in false beards or moustaches, I was now as well known in my disguises as I was without them.

Just as the train was starting to move and I was congratulating myself on securing an otherwise empty compartment, a young man with a large suitcase entered and sat down at the window seat opposite me. Apart from an initial glance in my direction, he was taking no notice of me at all, just staring out of the window as the train built up to cruising speed. But I, from behind my raised newspaper, was keeping my eye firmly on him; he had been in the ship's bar the previous evening, sitting alone across from me, and wearing the same short leather jacket and blue shirt.

He didn't look particularly dangerous: he was of no more than average height and probably weighed less than ten stone. However, in this business it's intelligence that makes the difference and he appeared to have no shortage of that commodity, judging by the resolute, but somewhat harrowed look in his clear blue eyes.

'Do you mind if I smoke?' he asked in a deep BBC voice with just a hint of an Ulster accent.

'Not at all. This is a smoker, you know.'

'Yes, I realise that,' he said, holding out a packet of Gallaher's Greens. I eyed him warily for a few seconds, then accepted the cigarette.

'Thanks.' Then, after we had lit up: 'Going to London?'

'Yes, Woolwich.'

'The Royal Artillery depot there?' I asked.

'That's right.'

I felt that if he were a soldier — and the shortness of his blond hair indicated that he was — then the fact that our paths had met twice could safely be put down to coincidence. Unless, of course, the SAS had been called in to deal with the Black Ring, and in view of Peppar's signal lack of success in that direction, I considered that to be a distinct possibility. I decided that this young man warranted further investigation. I said:

'I imagine it can be quite tricky being in the army at the present time, what with all these troubles going on and so forth. I mean a chap in your position . . .'

'Well, yes. I entered on an "S" type engagement — that's a short term commission — and the procedure was that I did my basic training with the regular recruits. As I soon found out, both the recruits and the instructors have a considerable hatred for any potential officer in their midst. Doubly so if he's Irish.'

'Yes, I can certainly sympathise with you on that score. Mind you, we wouldn't have stood for any of that nonsense during the war. Not in the SAS, anyway.'

'You were in the SAS?' he asked, as if seeing me in a new light.

'Oh, I think I can claim to have preceded Stirling in that little venture.'

'You mean you joined *before* Stirling?'

'In a manner of speaking, yes.' I had known he wouldn't believe me, but he was by no means unique in that. The main thing, however, was that I was making progress with my questioning. I said:

'When did you travel over?'

'Last night. You were sitting across from me in the bar.'

'Oh yes?' I started to chuckle. 'Did you see the run-in I had with that barman? I thought I was going to explode.'

'I'm surprised you made it past the security check-point,' he said, glancing up almost imperceptibly at my suitcase.

I think I gave a little start when he said this, then resisting an impulse to throw myself at him, I slipped my hand into my coat pocket and around the handle of the Saturday Night Special. Our eyes met, and as I stared into those cold blue depths I seemed to be seeing him for the first time. I wondered why I had failed to notice the calculating ruthlessness that was so apparent in his eyes and the set of his face. I said:

'So it's like that, is it?'

'What do you mean?' he said.

'Still, I'm surprised you've put your cards on the table so soon. What do you propose to do now?'

'I'm not sure —'

'Don't play games with me, sonny boy. I know why you're here — you've practically told me so yourself.'

Suddenly he jumped to his feet, his hands poised for action.

'Sit down,' I told him, pointing the revolver at his chest. His eyes showed surprise for no more than a second, then he gave a long slow smile and sat down.

'Murder on the Orient Express?' he said, apparently taking a light-hearted view of the situation; or, as was more likely, believing that circumstances were so firmly under his control that he could, for the time being, amuse himself at my expense. At any rate, I was finding his attitude distinctly disconcerting.

He said: 'I once read of a man in America who held up what they call a cigar store by pointing his finger at the assistant, cocking his thumb, and saying, "This is a stick-up!" Have you ever tried that approach?'

'Don't fool yourself this isn't a real gun. You might find out different.'

'It may interest you to know —'

'That's enough. Tell me who you're working for.'

'Myself, I should hope.'

'We don't have time for this. I'll ask you a direct question and you'd be well advised to answer it. Are you working for the Professor?'

'Not in the least,' he said, smiling. 'I'm sure the Professor has no need of my services. He has, I would imagine, quite an adequate supply of desperadoes at his disposal.'

'The authorities?'

This seemed to amuse him even more. 'Heaven forbid. I have just as great a contempt for the authorities as you seem to have.'

'So you *are* working for yourself?'

'In a manner of speaking, yes.'

I had considered knocking him unconscious then

making my escape at the next station, but I decided against that on the grounds that such action in what could be called a public place might well lead to my arrest, and at this stage of the game that would be disastrous. Moreover, I could not be certain that he did not have at hand, in the corridor or in the next compartment, a number of accomplices, waiting and listening for his signal. I said reluctantly:

'I suppose we can come to terms?'

He paused before answering to light a cigarette, at the same time seeming to ponder the advantages and disadvantages of coming to an agreement. He said:

'What's your best offer?'

'Five thousand.' He seemed surprised at this. I didn't know whether it was more than he had hoped for, or whether such a figure was unacceptably low for a man in his line of work. Finally he said:

'That'll be all right.'

Keeping my eye on him, I brought down and unlocked the suitcase, opening it in such a way that its contents were not visible to him. As I handed him the money I said:

'What put you on my trail?'

'Why, you did.'

'What do you mean?'

'Ah, that would be telling.'

A few minutes later the train began to reduce speed in preparation for its first stop. I decided to get off and do what I should have done in the first place, that is, hire a car. As I was leaving the compartment the young blighter said, either for my information or, as was more likely, to complete his victory over me:

'Oh, by the way, it's quite obvious that's not a real revolver. You can tell by looking at what's supposed to be the chamber. The entire replica has been moulded out of one piece of metal.'

Brooding over this early and unexpected reduction of my funds, I had not the slightest inclination to comment on the shortcomings of my Saturday Night Special.

Chapter 17

Grapplers from the East

The wife never liked London. She once said on an excursion we took together during the more amicable fifties that it was like Hell, the only difference being that London closes down at eleven o'clock. That's not to say she was lamenting the apparent lack of night life in that city — far from it. The act of staying up late to drink and perhaps forming one or two casual acquaintanceships fell firmly within the bounds of what she used to call 'promiscuous behaviour'.

And when such heavy condemnation fell upon the relatively innocent pursuit of night life, her attitude towards activities more directly sensual can easily be imagined; as can the fate of my efforts during the first phase of our marriage to initiate what was to me at that time a sophisticated sex life.

My London, however, never closes down. As a lifelong traveller along the more deviating paths that permeate society at all levels, I am usually able to get what I want at whatever time I want it — providing, of course, that sufficient funds are obtainable.

And I suppose that there is nothing like the acquisition, especially in an unorthodox fashion, of a very substantial sum of money to focus one's mind on the individual attractions that are available in a large city. A matter that so preoccupied me as I stood in the Dunwoody Hotel in Earls Court, waiting my turn to register, that I was not immediately aware of the minor commotion which was taking place at the other end of the lobby.

A stocky man with fierce eyes and a shaved head was having words with a young Japanese. Apparently, the stocky man — the manager as it turned out — had apprehended him in the act of taking a hamburger up to his room.

The Japanese, at first incredulous that this should not be allowed, now began to insist that he had a perfect right to convey such an article to his room: while the manager responded militantly that 'rights' of that nature, particularly those accommodating foreign habits, were not to be found in his hotel.

The altercation continued along these lines for several minutes, gradually becoming more heated as the manager's argument took a more personal turn, until, now red-faced with anger, he banged his fist on the desk and shouted: 'This is England, you know!'

Unable to refute that assertion, the Japanese mumbled something in his own language and walked away. Almost completely motionless, the manager glowered at him as he crossed the lobby and pointedly threw the hamburger into a waste-paper basket.

'That sounded nasty, dear,' said a woman behind

the desk.

'Nasty?' barked the manager, suspicion forming in his eyes. 'What was nasty?'

'What he said in foreign, dear.'

After looking swiftly around, he marched the length of the desk to face another Japanese who was standing behind me and glared at him as if expecting confirmation of the woman's remark. This elderly Japanese, a little discomforted by the manager's sudden and aggressive appearance before him, attempted to ease the situation by giving a weak smile and nodding his head. This was, I felt, intended as a gesture of politeness, and not as a confirmation of a remark which he may not have heard in the first place.

Meanwhile, the first Japanese had not only remained on the scene — perhaps his sense of honour demanded that he do so — but was standing at the bottom of the stairs describing a circle on his temple with his forefinger. A posture that was immediately abandoned when the manager, after crossing the lobby in four or five remarkably large strides, grabbed the Japanese by the throat and proceeded to choke him.

Now equally as red-faced as the manager, the Japanese started to punch him in the stomach with both hands, increasing tempo until his little arms were moving like pistons; a response which seemed to be not just inadequate but also, as I reflected upon the exposure this oriental almost certainly had to the non-pugilistic forms of the martial arts, surprisingly inappropriate.

The standard defence in this situation is, of course, a strong upward thrust with the forearms, followed immediately by a knee to the groin. A less effective response, but one certainly more fitting than this undisciplined punching, would be to break or weaken the manager's hold by tugging back sharply on his little fingers.

However, out of fairness to this Japanese, I did consider the fact that whereas some people experience a temporary sharpening of the faculties in the early stages of strangulation, most experience the opposite effect — and it was in this latter category that the Japanese obviously found himself.

Needless to say, I was reluctant to involve myself in any matter that might involve questioning by the police; however, when it reached the point that I was seriously despairing of the young man's life, I realised that I was in the position of being the only person able, or willing, to go to his aid.

So, positioning myself behind the manager, I placed my arms inside his own and with my knee in his back, broke his grip by dint of strong but not damaging pressure. He didn't struggle or say anything, just strode smartly away. And by the time I had dragged the Japanese to an armchair and assured myself of his continued existence, there was no sign of the stocky man with the shaved head.

There was also, I realised as I returned to the desk, no sign of the other Japanese and my suitcase.

It was of course a particularly dirty trick to walk off with a chap's property while he's saving someone's life; another example, I thought as I rushed about looking for my case, of how my good turns are so often used against me.

Returning from the street, I produced my Saturday Night Special and prodded the first Jap up to his room. That strangling carry-on was, I suggested to him, merely a ruse to distract my attention from the case.

He decided to play dumb, so I roughed him up a bit and left him to think it over with his hands and feet bound together and his necktie wrapped tight round his mouth.

My next call was on the manager, who was in his office, pouring himself a shot. But you can imagine the sense I got out of him. 'I've had trouble with you socialists before,' he said, rising furiously from his desk.

My left hook put paid to any ideas he had about getting his hands round my neck. It wasn't necessary to follow up with the right, but I was feeling very cross so I just let him have it.

I was on my knees, going through the manager's pockets for clues when Peppar and two heavies walked in.

It was one of the toughest interrogations I've ever sat through. As I was being led into an 'interview room' at the local nick, two electricians came out of it. It was probably their claw hammer that rested on the desk between Peppar and me, but it turned out to be a focus for my gaze during the four hours that followed.

There was this young soldier on the train who had a case similar to mine, I told Peppar, and I must have picked his up by mistake. It went without saying that I intended to hand it in after I discovered what was inside it, only this manager and two Japs got wind of it and were trying to stop me. It was a great weight off my mind to know that British Intelligence had got to the suitcase before them.

Peppar continued to caress the hammer. 'We didn't.'

'You didn't?' I repeated, not sure whether to believe him or not. 'You mean it really was the Jap?'

'Don't ask questions, Holland,' he snapped. 'Just answer them. Go back to the very beginning — take it slow and try to remember every detail.'

Relating for the third time the events of the past few weeks, I thought that Peppar was being unreasonable in drawing sinister conclusions whenever I said something that was inconsistent with my earlier versions. But that was all to the good: he became less aloof and began to challenge me with facts that were intended to discredit my story, which was exactly what I wanted because I was trying to pump him too.

Although the major was not inclined to answer my questions, he did mention McKaine's suspected connection with both the bank robbery and Black Ring. That came as no surprise to me, but I was taken back by his assertion that Dolan's motive for shooting at me was in no way related to the case. Dolan was out for revenge. Apparently, he was in prison when I helped put his step-brother away for blasting Dale Diamond; once released, he came looking for me. Peppar, noting his likeness to myself, paid him to impersonate me in an effort to flush out the Black Ring. That ruse was not successful.

He declined to comment on Portuguese Joe's contribution to the case, but I would say — going by the look of contempt on the major's face when I mentioned his name — that Joe was worse than useless.

Peppar did not accept that a facial likeness and a penchant for Jaguar cars were sufficient reason to identify McKaine as Billie's brother, whom I had kept under surveillance as a member of the Blackshirts during my own time in British Intelligence. Indeed, he even refused to accept the existence of the Professor.

'This Professor,' he stated, 'is nothing more than a figment of your strange imagination.'

'What about Faye, then?' I said.

He nodded. 'Yes, she's still missing — but not for the reason you give. We'll find her, just as we'll find McKaine.'

'Well, if I can be of any help to you,' I offered.

Peppar looked at me curiously. 'I'm afraid, Holland, that you may be otherwise occupied for a while.'

I waited for him to say it.

'Look, the police in Belfast wanted to slap you in prison for a thousand years. I insisted you stay at large, temporarily, because there was still a chance you would uncover something that was of use to me. That is no longer the case.' He rose slowly from his chair and walked to the door. Then, almost kindly: 'Goodbye, Holland.'

I sat there for some time, considering the unsatisfactory nature of my position. Then a constable entered and said, 'Come along, you.' I lifted my hat and went with him.

It was doubtless true that the Belfast police had wanted to charge me with at least one serious offence; however, after being returned to that city in the handcuffed custody of an RUC detective, I quickly formed the impression that not only were the police resentful of British Intelligence interference in matters which would normally fall under their jurisdiction but were reluctant to proceed with a case which, owing to Peppar's inept intrusion, had involved such deviation from normal procedure that a successful prosecution was strongly in doubt and, whatever the outcome, would probably result in a certain amount of embarrassment, if not censure, for the police themselves.

Whatever considerations may have weighed on their minds, the upshot was that I was not charged, and twenty-three days after that meeting with Portuguese Joe in the Ajax Cafe, I walked up the path to my house and, with more than the usual amount of trepidation, opened the door.

I didn't know if she was in, but I stepped gently, making no noise on the carpeted stairs and landing. As I opened the closet door to take out a change of clothes, there came a series of sharp cries from the next room. I listened for a few seconds, wondering if she might be in difficulties, then impelled, it must be admitted, more by curiosity than concern, I trod softly along to her room and opened the door.

For a few moments all I could see was a man's back, below which protruded two legs that I assumed belonged to my wife. As I was about to leave, he stopped thrusting and twisted slightly to look at me. It was now possible to see my wife's face and she obviously had saw mine, for her hand went up to her neck as she gasped something to her companion. Then her eyes closed and the arch collapsed, subjecting the white-faced man to an even greater indignity than that occasioned by my entrance. She had — if it is possible to do so in such a position — fainted.

'Didn't anybody see fit to tell the woman I wasn't dead?' I shouted at the ex-Hong Kong Police inspector, who had by now extricated himself and was hurriedly putting on his underpants.

'Not a very pleasant scene, it it?' I remarked. Then casting a last withering glance at my wife's naked and still motionless form, I turned and walked straight out of the house.

I walked for a long time: an aimless stroll that took me down the Ormeau Road, along Cromac and Oxford Streets to the Queen's Bridge, where I fed a sugar-topped bun to the seagulls; then west to High Street, below which runs the long since culverted River Farset, and south past the City Hall to the G&R train station. At Bradbury Place I was told off by a policewoman for crossing against her signal, then I went along Donegall Pass back to the Ormeau Road.

Outside my office I paused and looked for a few moments at a brown spill of paint on the pavement and the partially completed front that, new paint and old, was covered with a layer of grime. Then I unlocked the door and stepped inside.

There was a small hill of mail at the door, but that could wait for another day; as could my long short stories, my poem writing, the phone call to Gloria, the collection of Faye's Cortina and McKaine's Jaguar and, particularly, the cleaning-up of the office. Today, and for the forseeable future, I'd just drink Old Comber whiskey and smoke slow undisturbed pipes of Turkish tobacco, enclosing myself in a feeling of melancholic wistfulness when evening settled and below the bamboo blinds I caught glimpses of men and women returning to their homes.

Later on I'd have to consider what I was going to say about all this in *Case-Histories of a Soldier-Detective*. If anything, that is. My present feeling was that it might well be excluded on the grounds that since Portuguese Joe's approach was informal, I was not acting in my official capacity as a detective and did at no time represent Rapid Results Investigations.

MADAME EDDIE'S CHAMBER OF HORRORS

I expected the manager to be a hard geezer, but this one was round and soft all over. She swayed in wearing a cute black number and bounced over to the desk, parting her glossy red lips in a golden smile.

'The girl's only new,' she said, making a nice little flourish with her treble chins. 'But she'll understand what men like soon enough. Just give me twenty quid, ducks, and you can go down and see the lady with the scar.'

During the three minutes it took for Barney to make two orbits around his stomach, his stream of consciousness, expressed vocally only when he was in a reasonably upright position, resembled one of the darkest, most esoteric passages of *Finnegans Wake* . . .

'Ready to talk, Huggins?'

Barney's glasses had fallen off, but he could just about make out two seemingly enormous thighs towering up to a large black triangle. As he opened his mouth to speak, his teeth assumed that grotesque shape peculiar to people in upside down positions.

'I'm damned sure I am.'